PRAISE

"Jemc's subtle touch is evident in the focus and attention of *My Only Wife*. The reader's heart stirs and stops on her whim. This is a lovely, finely tuned book."

—Amelia Gray, author of *Threats, Museum of the Weird,* and *AM/PM*

"Jac Jemc's *My Only Wife* operates with the calm, pristine clarity of an enormous marble room. In moving, methodically arranged sentences, one comes across the surpassing surfaces and relics of a kind of intimacy that seems an increasingly difficult proposition to rightly preserve. At last, here is a novel concerned with timeless dedication, love, and respect, which phrased through Jac Jemc's steady warming eye needs no punch line or coincidence or cataclysm to give true glow to the glow itself."

—Blake Butler, author of *There Is No Year* and *Nothing: A Portrait*

"I adored this book. I adored the slippery, enigmatic wife of the title and I adored her adoring husband and I adored every lovely, heartbreaking sentence in this deftly written, beautiful book."

—Elizabeth Crane, author of *When the Messenger Is Hot* and *We Only Know So Much*

PRAISE FOR *THESE STRANGERS SHE'D INVITED*

"The word that kept coming to mind as I read this chapbook once and twice and a third time was 'impeccable.' The writing is quite crisp, almost intricate. Each sentence almost had an aphoristic quality."   —Roxane Gay, author of *An Untamed State* and *Ayiti*

"Each one seems a set piece, interchangeably, a curio on a slanting cabinet shelf, a mix of play and seriousness, a way of spooling up emotions and spinning them into tiny, hushed things. I would not be surprised to see this thing—poem, hybrid, flash?—alongside the gold-plated petrified bones of a deep sea fish or a looking glass or a dagger or a thimble made of crushed and varnished black bread or maybe even a type of large gleaming hook."

—Sean Lovelace, author of *Fog Gorgeous Stag*
and *How Some People Like Their Eggs*

"Smart, sharp chapbook. I felt pulled through each section seamlessly and ended up reading this three times in a row. 'Section 8' took the cake for me, but nothing disappointed here."

—Sarah Rose Etter, author of *Tongue Party*

A
Different
Bed Every
Time

A
Different
Bed Every
Time

Jac Jemc

DZANC
BOOKS

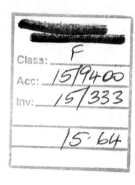

DZANC BOOKS

5220 Dexter Ann Arbor Rd.
Ann Arbor, MI 48103
www.dzancbooks.org

Designed by Steven Seighman

Library of Congress Cataloging-in-Publication Data

Jemc, Jac, 1983-
   [Short stories. Selections]
   A different bed every time / Jac Jemc.
      pages cm
   ISBN 978-1-936873-53-1
   I. Title.
   PS3610.E45A6 2014
   813'.6—dc23

                                                   2014013914

ISBN: 978-1936873531

First U.S. Edition: October 2014

Printed in the United States of America

10 9 8 7 6 5 4 3 2 1

To Jenny, for teaching me to read.

Contents

A Violence   1

The Grifted   7

The Dark Spot   11

Women in Wells   13

Marbles Loosed   17

Bent Back   21

Ratman   33

The Wrong Sister   35

Somebody Else's   41

Half   45

Judgment Day   49

Hammer, Damper   51

Unaccounted   57

The Crickets Try to Organize Themselves
Into Some Raucous Pentameter   61

A Heaven Gone   69

Like Lightning   73

Before We Pass This Way Again   75

The Chamber of the Enigma   81

The Colleens   85

Engrossed   87

The Direction of Forgetting   89

Roundabout the Bottom   93

Tangle   95

Points on Staying Alive During That Old War 97

Felted 101

Entered 103

A Willingness & Warning 105

More Mysteries 109

Twins, or Ambivalence 115

Prison Windows 117

The Tackiness of Souls 119

Hospitable Madness 129

Prowlers 131

Filch and Rot 137

Recipe for Her Absence 143

Both Fruit and Flower 145

Configuration 147

The Effects of Rotation 149

The Things Which Blind Us 151

Let Me Be Your Tugboat King 155

Alcyone 157

The Hush of the Party 159

Acknowledgments 165

Somebody once told me, as a thought in consolation, when you see a beautiful woman, always remember: somebody is tired of her.

—BARRY HANNAH, "TWO GONE OVER"

I do sense a life boarded up inside you.

—GARY LUTZ, "PARTIAL LIST OF PEOPLE TO BLEACH"

Anything that wasn't just totally accidental seemed wrong to me.

—EILEEN MYLES, *INFERNO*

A
Different
Bed Every
Time

A Violence

Every night I stunned myself with gin. On one date, a man and I ended up at the airport and ate rhinestones. We moved fast and real. The plane progressed in handfuls of miles at a time. I refused to keep secrets, but he told them to me anyway. After a few days of gorging under the guise of vacation, I hit the road, figuring out how to be kind. This man could rile me, lift me, convince me with his hands. It felt too much like a disadvantage.

Another man looked at me like I might gnaw off his face before dragging him into a bush. He calmed down and we shared a holy week of drinking. I suffered a hairline fracture, and every few minutes it felt like someone shot a hockey puck up my leg. We played sailors behaving badly. We skated on predictions of what might happen between us. I whispered in his ear, "I know what's beneath your pillow," and he asked me to repeat myself. We watched pig dissection on his computer and had bad dreams. By the end apologies were hovering around us, but neither of us could tell whose turn it was to speak, so we lost each other.

The next boy I met on a mission. My fingers fell asleep, a handful of beetles. He showed me a map and asked me to read it. When we finished, I applauded and we knew we would draw new cartographies on each other's skin. This news abstracted itself, refused to be comforting. I quieted bell after bell against my tongue. One night, fleshless, he emerged from the basement and began making accusations: *You are delirious. You are dungeoned. You are stapled shut.* I admitted my faults: *I am a drawer full of fire. Only a flash flood could put me out.* My appetite was pared. Starving myself of him did not feel like starving.

I slowed a little. I felt like I had made up for the lost time. I was all soft and crazy hair everywhere and boys paid me extra attention because they looked at me all the time like I'd just woken up beside them. But you can't go for it every time. You've got to dangle the carrot.

I kept running into men I'd dated while on dates with other men. I found new ways of explaining them to each other. Every time it happened I thought about how Wittgenstein called language a cage. I was living in a city that seemed smaller and smaller everyday. I had few deal breakers: I didn't trust hunters or jokes with punch lines. Beyond that I would allow myself to forget any vows I'd taken and looked forward to forgetting how many fingers I had on each hand. One guy kept insisting he was not hungry while we were watching a movie, but I caught him—twice—in the kitchen with a fork in his mouth. I developed moods that felt like they could be stretched forever like a piece of dirty bubblegum. Despite however much I tried to erase it, I had this human heart that was always showing up and milking itself into my body.

I made up things to say and tried to find the right person to say them to. *I am vibrating. I am beckoning. I have riddles for you.* Men with thick piano-key fingers. Men who offered to change light bulbs for me. Men made of glass and ones built of brick. Men who took me to concerts and tried to tilt their heads to mine. Men who the closer I got, the less I could see. Men who held me down when I asked and ones who just couldn't. Men with rabbit-hole grins and men with gruesome, peristaltic, nervous tics. I could watch each of them happen. I could see the wrongness. I could find beauty everywhere. When I woke each morning I could see that the day was capable of forking like the foot of a crow. I tried to remember where I'd been. I was sure I was smiling too much. Everything was funny. Deadlines moved themselves around me in a counter-clockwise direction. Every night I tried to figure out how to talk to someone new.

One night I went out with a gorgeous boy who had a brain in his head and kept trying to figure out what my faces meant, and I had to keep plucking his fingers from my mouth, against all of my desires. And I could feel that neither of us knew what to do with the yo-yo that was swinging between us and that both of us were fighting our collars with tugs and pinches. All around us, people were caring about each other, their hands finding other hands. He and I spent every minute of our time trying to forget the other one before we could remember them. He spun his straw around his glass and I was happy to have the distraction of watching the layers of liquid unstripe themselves. On this evening, I was fearful: it was easy to imagine spending years living alone, deep inside his body. I started trying to jigsaw him into my future. I fit the piece of him onto a big porch in the country, until I caught him flummoxing some girl at the next table. I told him I was ready to go. The conversation outside was a jumble of cigarettes and irreversibility.

At home I avoided my basement. I'd had a series of dreams of round teeth pushing through the gums of the doorway downstairs. I drew pictures diagonally on paper like women do and let the lines curl on themselves. I answered the door, unconcerned that my mouth, my hands, my dress were open. I put air in my tires like I might go somewhere. At six a.m., I'd tell myself, I will know if I will always be alone. I was never shy enough to wave goodbye; I'd just say it and mean it. I would watch the sky for stars rising slowly and evenly like car windows. I made my neighbor knock on my door while I was entertaining these men. I'd tell them it was my boyfriend coming home and shove them under the bed, just to keep things interesting.

I met a man at those chess tables in the park. The violent knocking down, the bold decisions, the small leaps that make statements. Every time we finished a game he convinced me to start another. He kept saying "polyglot" like it was something that showed up in a blood vessel. He threw up in the bushes on our walk to the café. When I asked if he was all right, he apologized for being nervous. I had thought he was just being an asshole. His mustache looked more like a horseshoe than a handle bar. Flecks of spittle clung near his mouth. He was balding, something I normally found sexy. While he said things I didn't care to hear, I imagined eighteenth-century children running toward us on the path, sticks nudging hoops ahead of them. When I tuned back in, it seemed he was trying to stretch my impression of him in another direction, but really it was snapping back opposite. At dinner, when he looked down into his bag to pull out his journal, I rolled my eyes—until he opened the book and a flyer for a strip club fell out showcasing a woman with star pasties, boots so tall the edges licked the folds of her labia. His hands crashed to his face before he turned to the potted plant beside him like he was going to wretch again. Instead his body seized several times and then relaxed. I picked up the flyer and said, "She is *pretty*," before the waiter took our order.

I drank too much coffee. The city felt like a pinball table, like I might slip between the sewer grates and become lost to the game.

I met a man at the natural history museum. I could tell by the way he pushed the buttons on the exhibits that we could have some fun. Each time the screen changed, another graph, another map, another face appeared, and he turned to see my reaction. I asked lots of questions about his life and no matter how I tried to fool him into being honest, he plumped the stories up so they sounded fancier. It was like seeing someone in the middle of a snowy field with no footsteps around them. Everyone has to get to where they are. I told him I didn't believe him and left him with the water birds.

I started to make questionable decisions. Crossing against the light. Crawling out windows onto porch rooftops in heels. At the amusement park I pulled the plush head off one of the workers wandering around in his cartoon costume. I got held for several hours, reprimanded, released, banned.

I allowed a spindly piece of a man to empty me of my bridesmaid dress. This gentleman in a good suit felt the urge to take that suit off, to put his glasses on the nightstand, to properly tell me the story of how he could touch me. I was veins and rich tastes in my mouth. I was gutsy and howling. I was a variety of surprises and I was wrong. I bared my teeth. I became a bird split open. Proximity, suspense and patterns clicked themselves together to try and predict the secrets of what lay ahead. I outweighed wisdom with pig-faced lust.

I started wearing my glasses all the time. I started wearing big clothes to make myself appear more vulnerable. I started dropping coins on the ground to get people's attention. I told myself, "I've changed." I asked men directly to my apartment and when they emerged through the front door I'd do my best to let my arms act as clothing. I was overrun with ghosts. I unfastened chains from morning till night. I spoke in lilting tones. I narrowed things down. Every angle was assaulting me. I tried to figure out if this was some kind of self-imposed death sentence. I stood outside closed doors and tried to make myself happy about it. My mind fulfilled with a basic conglomeration of faces, the specifics fading fast. Sometimes it was all I could do to be comforted by some vague ending glimmering in the distance. A slithering feeling constantly distracted me from the task at hand. I stared at a snail trying to curl its body into a coke bottle.

I left my windows wide open, and even in the pitch black, I imagined the people on the other side of the alley could see the glint off our bellies and backsides. They wondered, "Again?" They wondered, "How long?"

Over and over, until I felt different.

The Grifted

It was Saturday at the mansion. Grandfather had finished break-fast. It was Enza's day off and so I bussed the dishes to the kitch-en. "You've turned into a nice young man, Jim. You're sure to carry on the family name well. There's so much waiting for you," he called from the rear sun porch. I rinsed his plate and looked around. I tried to imagine more.

The doorbell rang.

In hindsight I'm sure she moved much more slowly. In the moment, though, as soon as I opened the door, the scam artist had her hand in my pocket, was leading me on a tour of my own home, starting with my bedroom.

"Trust me," she breathed in my ear, her hands sliding down my abdomen and robbing me of my shirt.

"Who are you?" I asked, and her face blossomed several tiny smiles.

"Let's just say my soul is full of guests." She looked around. "Do you have the time?" I was confused, excited, stupid. I point-ed to my watch on the dresser.

She grabbed it, scanned the face, and shoved it into a pocket before she lifted her dress over her head. She was on me, my clothes were off before I even registered the muffled clank of my watch against the floorboards. She worked her thumb into my mouth, fit her other hand into the stirrup of my collarbone, and pushed herself around. While she had me distracted, she examined the room for weak underbellies. She was good; I was gone and she was figuring out exactly where everything would be. I gathered myself snugly into some fantasy as she raided the surface of my desk from across the room. My face shut tight with my rising detachment until she forced a plea from me.

Her clothes were back on and she was up, wandering the room, opening doors and drawers before I'd even opened my eyes again. Her hands seemed full. I didn't ask her to leave.

My grandfather called my name.

"Are you Jimmy?" she asked with a mouth full of teeth. I nodded, unable to focus. "You should probably respond to whoever's down there calling you then, cowboy." I nodded again and she threw my pants at me. As I stretched my shirt over my head, I kept thinking, *carpetbag pockets, carpetbag pockets, carpetbag pockets.* Her hands closed around the collection of small liquor bottles I'd been gathering for years and when I heard them land inside her dress, the clatter sounded farther away than the bottom of her pocket. I kissed her neck, blindly, hesitated leaving her, not because I was afraid of why she was there, but because I thought she might be gone before I made it back.

When I reached Grandfather, he asked me to wheel him back inside before he asked who was at the door. "Just a canvasser," I lied. My lips felt swollen, roughed up. I wanted him to be able to tell. I could hear her steps above me. She was in Grandfather's room now. Something shattered. I heard the drag of wood against wood. Grandfather's hearing was almost gone, and he asked for his book. Everything in me sank with relief and I tried to pretend it hadn't.

I rushed back upstairs. The room in which I'd left her was empty. Only the bed, the dresser, a night table remained. The Tiffany lamp was missing, each drawer purged, the windows bare of their tapestry curtains.

I ran to Grandfather's room. The furniture was gone. The Oriental rug which had cloaked the ancient mahogany floors had been taken away. Holes hid in plain view where pictures, nails had once been. I shook my head, trying to startle everything back into view. My sight went blurry, looked more occupied for a second, then settled into emptiness.

I moved numbly to the library. There was nothing. Even the heat of the sunlight through the skylights was absent. I could hear her downstairs now, but I hadn't seen her pass me. How she must have moved.

I descended the service stairs, emerged in the kitchen, now the plain white interior of a box. No countertop, no pipes emerged where the sink had once run. There was only the rectangular absence of the doorway to the dining room. It felt hard to breathe, like the oxygen was fleeing the air.

The dining room loomed pitch black, and as soon as I walked through the doorway I could not even see the way back into the kitchen. No light stretched in. I could still hear the intruder ahead of me. I felt for the next doorway, but all I encountered was space. I tried to find a wall, but no matter how far I wandered, the only solid objects the room held were the floor and my feet. I heard the hard click of the heavy front door and moved towards it, but several minutes later, I had still not arrived. "Grandfather?" I called. The silence answered me firmly.

I was lost, exhausted, full, satisfied, alone.

When all you have is everything, the only thing left to desire is for every bit of it to be taken away.

The Dark Spot

By the fourth day I snuck into the smoky basement and pulled open the pressboard panel door of the furnace room. Cobwebs caught my forehead as I reached for the light chain. I pawed my face clean and cleared a path to the old weight bench that hadn't been moved in thirty years. Balanced on each end of the bar were old rubber Halloween masks: Death and the Wolfman, hidden from us as children because of how frighteningly realistic they were. "Happy Thanksgiving," I whispered to them before reminding myself that I'd come downstairs to be alone. I sat down and laid out a week's worth of yawns.

I'd spent the holiday clapping for every song my nieces performed, filling myself with apple desserts, and rehashing the plot points of past Thanksgivings with my sisters and parents.

I held my head in my hands and wondered if a hundred years in this filthy closet could be enough to undo the past few days. My inner eye zeroed in on an escape, but there were rides to be given to the airport in the morning, babies to be cuddled, dishes to be washed. The polite thing to do was stay.

I remembered that final holiday before anyone went away to college, or moved out of state, or spent Thanksgiving with a boyfriend's family. A distinguished year if only for the fact of our obliviousness of how easy everything would never be again. We dedicated the abundance of food and quarrels to the notion of family, and we did it with gusto. We daughters clinked our etched wineglasses filled with sparkling grape juice and made sure we looked everyone in the eye with our mischievous smirks. This was the last holiday I could remember without the nausea. After that, I started to feel ill from the pressure. From the feeling that everyone was supposed to live more on holidays, pack a year's worth of a relationship into several days, feel all that love and hate in such quick succession. It was all I could do to find the darkest spot in the house, the room where one of my sisters had grown penicillin on oranges back in junior high and where Halloween masks too scary for little girls were hidden out of sight, where I could sit and let my mind loosen.

I had tried to turn the weekend into a science, to make it into a game I could learn the rules for, to escape the cliché of it being difficult to be home for the holidays. If you asked me who I loved most in the world, the people I would list were under that roof, but spending four days with their adult selves, with the spouses they'd chosen and the children they'd wrought and the opinions they'd formed where curiosity had once lived, was more than I could manage.

Alone in the furnace room, I thought of a person trying to remember a phone number while someone else shouted random numbers in their ear. I thought of trying to sync three clocks perfectly with only two hands. I thought of impossible pulses.

There are times when I know I'm a part of something, even when I'm not actively adding to that thing. Like the dim spot on a fluorescent sign, I can feel the other sections buzzing around me, and I know people can make sense of the words, because the light of the working parts is enough. They can fill in that dark gap because they know what *should* be there. And sometimes the hardest thing is to be recognized as a part of something that I know I had nothing to do with, no matter how much I wish I did.

Women in Wells

The certainty clings to his smile from the minute she opens the door. They stare at each other recognizing bits that have faded and others that have taken shape over the years. She makes some indecipherable gesture with her eyes, breaking the connection, and laughs. "You're too good to be true. They'll be home soon, I think. I'll wait with you."

He comes in, thankfully unable to think up an excuse not to. She puts on a record and asks if he wants something to drink. He nods, and when she leaves the room he sits. Everything around him is older now and the same. He remembers playing here as a child, with these brothers who are due back any minute. These brothers and this sister of theirs haven't changed the house at all since their grandparents died. He breathes in the smell of mothballs. The scent comes from all sides.

When she returns, the glass looks dusty, and he sets it on a coaster. The soul music on the turntable hustles a circus into her muscles and he sits watching her dance, watching the glimmer of her watch face can-can around the room.

It's taken him a moment to figure it out, but this girl reminds him of someone. She reminds him of that woman in the well when he was a child, just up the road. That woman he told no one about, who'd spoken to him calmly, who'd seemed not happy but certain of her place all the way down there; that woman who'd just stopped speaking to him one day. No flashlight could shine far enough to see if she had gotten free or if she was just being quiet, and he couldn't tell anyone she'd stopped talking to him because they'd wonder why he never tried to help her out. This girl who answered the door? Who said just a few words as she let him in? This girl who he's known forever, but not for a while? The voice this girl grew into is the voice of that woman in the well.

All the while she dances, trying not to color so exactly between the lines, slapping the walls. She wonders, beneath the beat, if this man won't get up and join her; what could he possibly be thinking about her while she willows and swipes around the room?

The music slows and she calms herself and sits in the rocking chair. This man, here. Her brothers, nowhere. This girl can't be still and because she can't be still? She begins to whip her tongue around her mouth, counting her teeth: twenty-eight. Wasn't she supposed to have thirty-two? The number thirty-two sticks out in her mind.

He watches her, the lump moving under her jaw skin, and thinks about how he still sees her as a girl. But she's beyond that. Surely puberty has wrenched its way through her system and, by now, established well-worn patterns. She is still lithe, pale-looking. Girl-like. They both have evidence in their minds of the other being younger.

He wants to hear that voice again. For years his pride has named itself plainly around pretty girls, but with this one, each thing he thinks to say seems a high-handed sermon delivered from beneath a cartoon mask. He distracts himself with the newspaper from last Sunday lying on the coffee table. He leafs through to the crossword and fills in a few squares. He looks up at her and finds her eyes. He never saw the woman in the well, but he knows this is how she looked up at the silhouette of him against the daylight. Disconcerted, he reads her the next crossword clue: "River in which the heroine of *The Scamps of London* drowns?" This girl? She hums her elegiac response, lowly, "The Thames."

He escapes behind the crossword again, eager to hide his excitement at hearing her voice. Yes, that was it. He is sure now. It is full and vacant in the same ways as the voice of the woman in the well. How funnily life was able to fold on itself.

She tucks her feet up into the chair, happy to have company but wasting the opportunity to make legendary decisions. She peels her nails and thinks of where her brothers might be. Until this guest had arrived, she'd repeated a mantra from nowhere, again and again, out loud at first, until it wouldn't stop itself even in the silence: "To become abandoned, you've only to extinct the others." These aphorisms had been showing up for months now. She watches the window, sure her brothers will pucker into focus at any moment.

The man will shift on the couch, squeaking against the plastic cover, and pretend to look at the newspaper while he threads her voice through his head. The girl will rip off the tips of her nails one by one and the same sentence will travel quietly into and out of her mouth. She will salivate and swallow it whole.

These two will be in this room together for hours, and what originally felt like a solitary stubbornness, slowly, will show itself to be spineless. The brothers will arrive back, with apologies. The girl will retreat, and the visitor will never admit what he's heard.

Marbles Loosed

The question I asked myself was simple: How is it that someone can be lost in a system that exists for keeping track?

When I was a child, people told me I had pearl eyes. I'd rub my sandy fingers in them, sure that was the only way to keep them smooth and beautiful.

I don't remember my momma, but I remember being kept warm on dark, windy beaches, and I know that must have been her. If you're asking if I remember her face though? No.

I remember the face of my first home after her. I remember because I had to decipher it, so I could predict when it was time to run and when it was time to hold still. I remember that face thinking I should know more than I did, and punishing me for it.

I remember the pink, pulpy flower face of my grandma. She didn't try too long to keep me. It took them a while to find her, and when they did, she required convincing to think with her own mind that I was hers. On the first day, she called me Little Bird, but by the second she'd started seeing her daughter in me, and the darkness dipped in.

I remember the expiring Phoebe family who took me in, all of them withering like they'd gone without for too long. How they convinced the state they could stand another child was beyond me, but then my roots were shallow, and they were getting more cash than the raising of me required.

I imagined myself a velvet bag of marbles loosed on a hardwood floor. I'd been scattered so quickly that there was no time to think about what direction to go. Now, I try to look back at my childhood to remember, but it's hard to pick out moments. Every time I was placed with a new family was just a layer of the time before.

I remember the kingdom of heaven and finger touches on my forehead, like belief could seep through my skin, deep into my brain coils, and me asking questions and being told the Lord would provide any answers I needed, and scowling at being denied the opportunity to learn.

I remember listening to phone calls the blond one made to my case worker, lie-telling about some capsules she planted in my bag, and me, too young and too shy to know how to pin it back on her, but then if I won that case, if I proved I wasn't lying, the outcome would be no different—either way they were putting me in another home, and that's what everyone wanted.

I remember what it was to be read stories before bed, and hearing about how Goldilocks found a house where she didn't belong, but before the bear family kicked her out, she at least got some warm food and a good nap in. I remember believing that story more than the other fairy tales, because there was no happily ever after, just Goldie running off into the woods and the bears left to deal with the feelings of their privacy having been breached.

There were houses with locks on the insides of rooms and houses with locks on the outside, and I was used to feeling trapped either way.

I remember outgrowing clothes and repairing split seams myself, my shirt getting a little smaller each time I sewed it shut. I tried to swipe dresses from my sisters, from my foster mom, but they'd swipe them back and so I'd eat little of what was put in front of me for dinner, in the hopes of better fitting the clothes the next day.

I remember the man who would play the drums in the night. I'd go downstairs to tell him I couldn't sleep, and he'd beckon for me to come closer. He'd breathe his warm beer breath on my head while he hugged me and said he was sorry. After I'd tucked myself back in, the rhythms would start again.

An instant's rallying glow is numbed when you dwell too low. I remember, after a hard rain that broke through the roof, being forced out onto the earth, and the wind wearing away half of my complexion. I began with an old-fashioned heart, but it was demolished every time I dropped it out of myself in purple syllables. I grew hard.

I remember the family that put the video tapes back in the wrong cases. When I thought I was going to watch a cartoon, panting men and shrieking women filled the screen with all of their skin-colored shapes.

I remember my teeth falling out my head and no one telling me they would grow back bigger and stronger. I remember trying to match my mind to each home and thinking it wasn't normal to adjust my opinions so much. I remember learning the continents for school and thinking that if you define something big enough, it's harder to recognize the changes.

It's tough to remember the individuals that housed me, but I can rattle 'em off in order easy. I listened to a radio story about men who memorize the order of a shuffled deck of playing cards. They can memorize and recite each card in under two minutes, but ask 'em to tell you where the queen of diamonds is and they'd stare blankly back at you. That felt familiar.

I remember the moment I learned that one day they'd believe I was capable of caring for myself, and I remember the counting. I remember running away, trying to prove I knew better. I remember being brought back, and knowing it would only be days before they'd find a new home where they could lose me again.

Bent Back

At fourteen they diagnosed me with scoliosis, which basically meant my spine kept trying to sneak west. My parents had drained their bank account in a series of bad investments. My uncle, who'd cajoled my mother and father into the first round of some doofus's pyramid scheme, had recently thrown himself off the Golden Gate Bridge. That doesn't seem like an especially original way to die until you consider that we all live in Chicago and he had to buy a plane ticket to get himself that far.

The doctors thought the curve in my back was minor enough that it could be effectively treated with a brace. No surgery would be needed if we acted quickly. My parents paid for the brace with money they didn't have and trusted me to use it while they carried on with their strange, self-obsessed performance of financial grief. Every night my mother rebalanced the budget, artfully arranging her ledger, bills, and adding machine on the dining room table, while my father wasted cash at the bar on the corner. It seemed like part of being married was promising to be blind sometimes.

I wore the brace around the house, out the front door, and back in, but by the time I got to school each day, I'd crumpled the brace into a duffle bag I carried in addition to my backpack. I could tell the sway was worsening, but no one else was watching. In gym class doing side bends, I could slap my left palm flat on the floor, but when I pulled myself over to the right, I could barely knock my head parallel to the ground.

My sister, five years older than me, had just been admitted to the Art Institute and couldn't get enough of painting pictures of my screwy spine. I took my shirt off for her almost every day, forgetting about awkward adolescence, but she exaggerated the bow from the start and when it started looking more and more like her pictures, she never even noticed. When I absented myself from her studio in the garage, she worked on paintings of wigs and the legs of little girls younger than me. I don't think I'd even gotten my first period. I still powdered my armpits with talcum, just to have some responsibility, not because I needed to.

I suppose, looking back, I was making some sort of attention grab by not wearing the brace, but spines don't warp that quickly. My attempt performed more of a sleight of hand than a leap through a flaming hoop. I hoped someone would notice and care for me or about me. I searched for truths.

My sister played her sad music loudly as she painted me and I knew that biology was preparing to rip its way through my system and change everything.

I'd always been an entrepreneur of sorts: lemonade stands, dog walking, friendship bracelets. I'd also started sliding cigarettes from my father's packs one at a time. I'd carry them in a special case in my backpack and sell them to the kids at school for a dollar. I never smoked one myself. I feared stunting my growth— ironic to say the least. I'd been saving up the dollars for a puppy. I'd done my research and began visiting the pound on my way home from school almost every other day on the lookout for a dog worthy of my care. I found a mangy mutt of a thing, young but not so cute that anyone else liked him. I knew my parents wouldn't pay for the supplies or the dog's shots, what with their monetary anguish, so I was waiting until I had a critical mass of singles in a roll. Then I would unveil my hard-earned dollars and show them that I had saved up enough to care for a dog for a whole year. I hadn't figured out yet how to explain how I'd earned the money. I worried they'd accuse me of stealing right from their wallets and demand I give the cash back. The thought of the added step of stealing and selling the cigarettes being totally worthless drove me wild with injustice. My parents would grab back the fistful of dollars and I'd have to live knowing I'd aided my fellow students in the accrual of a deadly habit.

On Sundays my mother dragged my sister and me to church. I mostly ignored everything that went on and daydreamed about boys and dogs and what would happen when my parents finally found me out in public without that brace on.

My favorite part was when the congregation would recite the longer prayers together. There were slight variations depending on the versions they learned and when the congregation's mouths touched different words at the same time, I could never decide if the result sounded like a beautiful chord or an argument. I stared up at the cross and thought about how Christ had known what was coming and how he must have mentally prepared himself for a long day.

My sister seemed suddenly enthralled by mass. We left and she tried to point out all of the loopholes to my mother, and my mother just kept repeating the sentence, "That's faith."

On the way home from church my mother stopped to give communion to an older parishioner. My sister and I sat in the swing on the shut-in's front porch and played word association games.

"Heave."

"Heavy."

"Weeping."

"George."

"Oooo, who's George?" my sister asked, and I had to explain how I'd connected "While My Guitar Gently Weeps" to George Harrison.

When we got home, I couldn't take my church clothes off quickly enough. I stood in front of the mirror, unbuttoning, and wondered how I could be tired by noon on a Sunday. I stripped down to just my underwear and the brace, and poked at the spots where the hard plastic made my flesh bulge out. "You're not fat," I told myself. "Shut up."

I went out to the yard with a book and a blanket, kneeled on a bright fig and watched the juices blossom through the throw.

I jotted down the dreams I could remember and when I re-read them, they sounded like apologies to myself: consoling, re-assuring, "won't let it happen again." I laid in the sun, still, and searched inside my body for the sensation of each organ pumping me alive.

The day was breezy and I climbed to a low tree branch, closed my eyes and held my arms straight out to the side, feeling the air and the leaves reach for the sensitive skin of my inner elbows and the spot my tank tops left bare between the brace and my arm-pits. My father strolled by with hedge clippers.

"You look like a bird."

"Good," I said, squinting one eye open to see if he lingered.

I could tell my father had the same thought every day of his life: how did I make these two weirdos?

My sister had been dabbling in performance art then, rehearsing her new piece: resting her chin on the dining room table, try-ing to prevent a rat from throwing itself over the edge with her cupped hands.

"Cecile," I said, "I'm done with my homework, if you want me to pose."

She scooped up the rat and put him in his tank. On the way to the garage, she ran her hands through her hair before washing them.

"Becky, you're a real natural. I swear. No one with an effed up back has been so paint-worthy since Frida Kahlo."

"Rebecca," I said to her. "I want people to call me Rebecca now."

"Yeah, right on. Reinvent yourself, kid. I'm into it. How's the puppy fundraising?"

No one else knew about my silent theft and clandestine sales. She liked the idea. We thought I might just single-handedly wean our father off cigarettes. We knew that wasn't possible, of course, but we had all sorts of justifying to do.

"It's going well. I'm about a hundred dollars short," I said, patting the back pocket of my jeans. I kept the money on me, sure my mother would find it if I left it in my room.

"Here's something I bet you haven't thought about: what happens if you want to go away to school? What do you do with the dog then?"

"I'd take it with me, *obviously*," I said.

"*Rebecca*, you can't have a dog in a dorm room," she said.

"Dad told me I look like a bird."

"That's sweet?"

"I don't think it was meant to be. But I liked it, yeah."

She hummed and continued painting.

"Have you ever slow-danced, Cecile?" I asked my sister.

"Yes, of course," she answered.

"Like with someone you really like?"

"Yeah, I guess. What's going on? Do you have a dance coming up?"

"Probably at the end of the year."

"It's so not a big deal, Becs. Just a body against a body."

"*Rebecca*," I corrected her.

Several days later my sister asked me back to the garage. The warm spell had drooped. She wanted to try a slight variation on a piece she'd made a few weeks earlier. She needed my head at a different angle and hadn't had luck painting it without me there.

Cecile got things ready while I wandered her studio, which sat full of our old bikes and the sled, the gardening tools, bags of soil.

"Cecile? Why is there a goldfish in the washbasin?"

"Oh, Bruno won it for me at the Mt. Carmel carnival. I don't have a bowl yet." She coughed.

"Bruno? Who's Bruno?" I flicked at the water a little to make the fish swim. "You can't leave a fish in a sink covered in your old paint. Carnival fish are doomed as it is. Give the little guy a chance."

"Bruno is my new *friend*."

"I *see*. What were you doing at Mt. Carmel anyway? You know all the money they earn from that carnival goes to the church, right? I thought you weren't into that."

"Mom asked if I wanted to go to the novena with her. I think she was joking, but I told her I'd come with and hang out at the carnival until the novena was over and then we could ride the Ferris wheel like old times."

"Really going for Daughter of the Month, huh? Why didn't you ask if I wanted to come with?"

"Aw, Becs. I thought it might make you sad. That you can't ride so many of the rides now."

I sighed. No one was taking to my request to be called by my full name.

"And, besides, I think it was meant to be that I wandered alone for a while, because I met Bruno."

"Tell me more about this Bruno."

"He graduated from Lane too. He's taking some time off deciding what to do for college. Right now he works as a projectionist at a movie theater on Western. He's a real dude, but I talked to him about my art and he seemed really into it." She paused to cough. "I was taking a bunch of photographs that night with plans to use some for paintings. Wanna see? Come here. I'll show you."

I wandered over to her laptop set up on an old door balanced on two sawhorses. Bruno filled the screen. He was no one I would picture my sister with. He had on a Sox T-shirt and baseball cap. "This is the guy who won you the fish?"

"Yup, I named the fish Bear in his honor."

"That's really special, Cecile." I rolled my eyes, and she shoved me.

"Quit it, Becky. He's really sweet and he's actually super smart. He knows so much about movies and reads the *Trib* everyday. He's way up on current events. He made *me* feel dumb with how little I knew about Chicago politics."

"Awesome. I only hope I can find someone to make me feel stupid some day."

"Oh, Lord. Fine. I don't know when you got so cynical, kid. I'm going to invite him to dinner at home here next week. You're gonna have to be nice."

"Good luck with that," I said, taking my shirt off and easing onto the stool set up for me.

Cecile cranked some sad song and I heard her scrape another cough out of her throat. She'd been smoking. Suddenly I knew.

When I walked into the dining room the next day, there was a pigeon chained to the table. Every few seconds it'd remember it was trapped and flap its wings frantically. I had no desire to watch that bird pull its own foot off. "Cecile!" I hollered. This was too much. She wandered downstairs, stretching, rubbing her eyes. "Cecile," I said, "we live in Chicago, not the fucking country."

"Whoa, Becs. Language!"

"Seriously though, this bird's life is not some trial you get to put it through. It's a living thing and deserves to be free like you and me."

"Life is a miracle. Blah, blah, blah."

"This bird is shitting all over the dining room table, Cecile."

"Eh, she's fun to be arouuund," Cecile drawled.

"What is wrong with you? Are your drunk or high or something? What is the deal?"

"Aw, God! I am going back to sleep, *Rebecca*. This is too much. You are *not* my mother. Jesus."

I wasn't, but I was the closest thing she had right now and vice versa. Our mother had taken up a second job catering in the evenings and on weekends, and we were lucky if we caught her for the minute it took her to brush her teeth twice a day to babble news at her or ask for lunch money.

"You used to be fun!" Cecile called from halfway up the stairs. When she reached the top. I heard her kick something. A second later the punch bowl shattered down the stairs. She'd brought it up there to soak her feet a few nights ago and now the crystal stretched itself down to the hallway.

I sat at the table and said everything I had to say by tapping my fingernails on the surface.

My mother stopped home between catering shifts to grab a clean white shirt and I asked her how she liked the bird chained to the dining room table.

"There are moments when all I can think about are dead birds in the dark, Becky. I'm mostly unconcerned."

"That's where we get it from, I guess," I said and wandered away, her voice sticking in my ears.

I went to the kitchen and started pitching expired jars of condiments into a trash bag. I tried to haul it out to the alley, but the bag broke, leaving me more lopsided than usual and nauseated. I wasn't supposed to carry such heavy loads without the brace on, so I went back inside for a couple more bags. I cleaned up the mess and divided the trash between the new sacks. When I opened the back gate, Bruno had a knife to my throat and I dropped the bags again.

"Give me the money!"

I reached into my back pocket and pulled out the wad of singles I'd been saving for the puppy. I handed it over without a thought. All of this felt right. I shook my head, angry at myself for having the cash on me, but relieved to give it up. "That's all you want, right, Bruno? Don't mess this up."

The blade dug into my skin. Not enough to make me bleed, but I could tell he didn't like that I knew his name.

"I won't tell her. Do you want me to call Cecile down here? I can tell you she's not in a real good mood. She wouldn't unchain the bird in the dining room and she kicked a punch bowl down the stairs."

"What are you talking about, kid?" he asked. He took the knife away from my skin and shoved the cash into his own pocket. He had a wide ugly forehead his baseball cap had covered in the photograph; his eyes were useless nickels in his head. I didn't say anything and let the silence crumble his resolve. I wished something would happen.

"Cecile!" I shouted over my shoulder and her face appeared in the window. "Bruno's here!" I screamed through the glass. She smiled and disappeared to run down the stairs.

I told Bruno to put the knife away. "I hope you at least buy Cecile something with that. Nothing living. She can't sustain growth."

Bruno grimaced. Cecile flung her arms around him and they mashed their tongues together. I figured manners had no place here, so I stuck around, waiting for an introduction, until I couldn't stand it.

"Cecile, will you take this trash out? I've gotta go." Without taking her mouth off his, she pointed a thumbs up my way.

Cecile's solo show finally opened: sixteen portraits of my spine pointing in all different directions. She treated me like some side-show act when I appeared at the gallery, parading me around to all of her friends with their unkempt hair and lack of antiperspirant. I excused myself, not following the conversation, unable to participate in the unbridled praise comparing Cecile to name after name I'd never heard before.

Bruno stood at the snack table across the room, looking out of place in a basketball jersey and jean shorts drooping below his butt. I walked toward him and he tried to slip away, but a gaggle of professors were clumped between him and the rest of the room.

"Hey, Bruno. Still living the dream, huh? Did you buy something nice?"

"I still don't know what you're talking about, Rebecca," he said, and I had to blink back instant tears. I'd never wished someone would call me Becky so badly in my life.

"Let me know if you need any more cash," I choked out and turned away.

Cecile had begged our parents not to come, but there they were, ogling the paintings, toggling their eyes between them and the real-life me, sizing up what they'd been ignoring. My mother and father stared at me, my mother inspecting my torso to try and tell if I had the brace on under my sweater without actually having to ask me. They expected me to start making excuses any second. The feeling was mutual.

Ratman

I arrive back from visiting my mother for a week on September 12th. Magpie gives me a live rat as a welcome-home gift. He never gets it right. No matter how hard I try, I will never be able to position my target closer to where he is pointing his arrow. I know he thinks he's aiming straight for me, and sometimes I find myself capable of thinking this is endearing. He holds the rat in his dirty, browned hands and looks at me like I should know how to look back at him. Eight years ago, Magpie wanted to have sex on September 11th. Like *the* September 11th. I wasn't into it, but I kept trying to convince myself that it could help, that it could make us feel like we weren't alone or in danger. Magpie fucked me on a pile of old newspapers, my bare ass rubbing the newsprint, Magpie squeezing tight at my hips. I tried to forget the dirt under his fingernails, how it seemed like they never got clean. The whole time, the pile of dry paper wobbling, I kept thinking about the tremor of a building before it falls. I kept thinking of steady streams of cigarette smoke. I kept thinking of kindling.

I smiled at Magpie, because I thought that would be nice, but he had his eyes crimped shut, busy thinking of someone else, imagining the cushion of *her* breasts against him as he rocked into her, busy thinking of the soft landing of a safety net, of some set of primitive wall drawings that would affirm his sense of being right where he belonged. I made estimations. I thought of Zeno's paradox. I guessed at what the halfway point would be. Then I guessed again. And then again. And then, contrary to the rules, Magpie arrived, but I was still only half of half of halfway there. He slumped against me and I bumped my head on the wall behind us and Magpie didn't notice. This September 12th, Magpie followed me around the house with the rat clutched to his chest until he squeezed it too hard, and then we had several ounces of dead flesh and limp tail to deal with, and I wondered what made me come back and come back and come back. Magpie cried on September 12th. I had never seen tears come from him before. I tried to appreciate the gestures, the rat and the tears, once I realized I didn't have to deal with them. I measured our life together and divided and divided and divided, and though I felt like I was making it smaller, in reality I was metastasizing it. Magpie looked at me in that way that wanted me to look the same way back, but finally, I looked away.

The Wrong Sister

Okay. Say the reason you're stuck here in limbo is totally unclear to you. Say you were a woman who cared about little but treated others basically well. Say you had a twin who was married to a doctor, but because you were so ambivalent, you never agreed to partner up, never liked anyone enough to commit or even give someone a real chance, to ever approach the situation where you might have to explain these feelings to another human being because you've joined to have and to hold, in sickness and in blah blah blah…

But every once in a while, because it seems harmless and because sometimes your sister needs a break and because you gave up on that theater degree long ago but miss the thrill of lying, of being genuinely dishonest—let's say ever year or two you relieve your sister, and unbeknownst to her husband you replace her for a week or two, tops. Your sister's husband is the most crass and unpolished doctor you've ever met. He's a rube with a medical degree. You don't even recall the branch of medicine, so uninvolved and detached are your interactions even when you're pretending to be his wife. Somehow this man is actually a really good doctor—top of his field, full of expertise.

You live in a big city in a small neighborhood when you're playing his wifey. When you're you, you live on the other side of town. No one really knows you. The grocery store clerk might recognize you if you smiled at her once in a while, but as earlier stated, you're a bit heartless, so you haven't. Most people who see you assume you're your sister on a bad day. Let's say your sister comes to you and tells you her husband's really in a mood lately and though she still loves him, to be around him right now is to tear her hair out. "Please," she says, "be me."

You shrug. Agree to it. Let her know what's going on at work, switch cell phones, squeeze into those pointy-toed shoes she thinks are chic, erase yourself into her. Drive in her car, to her house, and get ready for a week off. Cook some lobsters for dinner, listen to their screams without interest. Smile at the rooftop garden, at her husband's color-coded tie rack, at that godforsaken dog confined to the laundry room.

When her husband gets home, you know what she means immediately: he's acting up. His eyes clock around, avoiding your face, landing on it at every quarter hour and ticking away. His facial hair seems mangy and patchy—like he's been letting the razor slide around willy-nilly. He unloads groceries and you're surprised he's done shopping. This doesn't seem like him, but then you see that it's nothing to be floored by: ten pounds of center-cut rib-eye, two hundred massive garbage bags, straws, beef jerky, a box of donuts. You look at him, and in your best impersonation of your sister, you say, "What the hell is all this?" He grabs the bundle of zip ties from you, and replies curtly that it's stuff he needed from the store that you (your sister) had not gotten for him. You pluck the lobster from the warmer and say, "Dinner, mon cher, is served." He plops himself down and before you have properly buttered your meal, he's inhaled his and is heading towards the garage.

"You're welcome," you call, and his response is an insouciant "Fuck you."

You know what's going to happen before it does, and you don't do anything to stop it. He's down in the garage with his supplies defining the margins of his sanity. He's making illegible decisions and convincing himself he'll decipher the handwriting later. Here is your sister's husband, your husband, for the sake of the rest of the story, and he's planning her demise, your demise, accordingly. And you know it'll be complicated for your sister when all of this unravels: but there're no children involved so you say, "What the hell?"

You wonder about your sister blaming herself but figure she'd rather feel guilty than dead. You, however, are ambivalent. Here's what will happen. Your husband will come upstairs and apologize. He'll ask if you want to go get a drink. He's had a wretched week. You'll say, "Where?" He'll say, "How about we just head around the corner to Ray's?" You'll say, "Sure," and head for the garage. He'll rush after you, pull your arm, suggest you just walk. The car's been acting funny. You can imagine what he's got laid out in preparation in the garage already. Trash bags, cutting tools. If he's smart: some lye.

God love this man and his nutty streaks. He has no idea anyone is on to him, least of all his victim. You think how foolish he is to do it in the garage—the concrete will stain—but it's not your problem. You think of calling your sister and saying something cryptic that might ease her guilt after the fact, but decide it might be too fishy. You want her free and clear of this nut job ASAP.

Birds glide beneath your skin. For a moment, you think, who's the nut now? You're convinced this joker's gonna kill you tonight.

What? Suddenly you're clairvoyant? But you know too well; he has that calm about him where he's sure of himself and he doesn't need to do any convincing—he just needs to let the story unravel.

The birds keep chirping, but you're still convinced you cannot get gone enough. He's sure this will solve all his problems, but you know this gesture will be read like a wasteland. It doesn't matter what's been or what will be. Tenses have been paved over.

Say you walk to Ray's. You sneak to the bathroom. You examine your face in the mirror. You're pretty sure you don't believe in an afterlife, but in the event there is such a thing, who knows if you'll be able to see anything, much less your own face. You look at the blue flame–tinted circles beneath your eyes. You think of all the deaths you've avoided: the canoe trip in the storm, the mugging, that time your appendix jammed itself huge into the rest of you. All incongruous warnings for the decision you're making right now.

You look a little longer. No, you're not getting sentimental, but you want to make sure there's enough time for the sedative to dissolve in your drink. You don't want to wake too early to a gray foggy cloud of your own bright scarlet. You don't want to see the brownish tint of you as the yellow pages sop up your gore.

You emerge, and the bartender gives you a look like he has a secret he knows he should tell you, but you look away quickly so he doesn't feel implicated. The whiskey barks down your throat all familiar-like, but husband is all fanned eyebrows and tilted breath.

You gulp the drink down and smile at husband and bring his hand to your mouth for a kiss. It is sweaty, but you make nothing of it.

The rest is blurry: you get loopy and other patrons notice. Husband takes you home. He butchers your somnolent self like a fine-boned rabbit. He flushes fourteen pounds of you down the toilet. He files a missing person's report and your sister grows confused. They never find the rest of you.

Stories start coming out around the neighborhood: large purchases of rubber gloves, trash bags, knives and saws. A regular at Ray's says he saw the two of you there and tells how you'd gotten wiped out with one glass of whiskey. Husband's office reports missing quantities of sedation samples.

The police find the wad of your muscle and fat in the septic tank, but your husband's lawyer argues a person could survive the loss of this much flesh. He charms the grand jury into thinking the evidence is inconclusive. Turns out it doesn't matter if people recognize you buying the damning supplies. Husband remains a practicing physician in the free world. Your sister can see what happened, and as soon as the trial is over, she runs as far away as possible to start a new life.

About a day after you're chopped to bits, you wake up in some mental state at Ray's, bodiless. "This must be the ghost life," you think. But you never cared about anything. What could you have to settle? And here? Say this boredom is eternal. "Well, then," you think half-heartedly, "all these men are stuck smoking with the wrong sister."

Somebody Else's

Looking back, it's hard not to feel crusted. When I press on those memories they exhale a dusty hiss. I showed up on the set and had my lightly padded skeleton sewn into some lint ball of a sweater. The episode was set in a ski resort, the town heavy with snow and trapping everyone in the lodge. Of course, all of it was filmed on a studio lot in California and cut with some stock footage of a ski lift climbing a mountain. My character was just supposed to be sitting by the fireplace when Larry walked in to show his cousin Balki how to pick up a lady. His line was, "Would you like some coocoo?" The character wanted to say "cocoa," but was so nervous to talk to me that it came out "coocoo." I was supposed to say, "I think I've had enough, thanks!" and stalk off, a suspicious shell of a woman.

All went according to plan, and I waited anxiously for the episode to air, for my agent's calls to increase in frequency. But the episode came and went, and the phone never rang. I guess I could have kept trying, but if I wanted to, I would have, or at least that's what a book told me.

I started to stay home, watching the old movies I'd grown up with—suspense thrillers and musicals and dramas about aging film stars being replaced by younger ones. I reached into the gap between the cushions of my couch to find change to tip delivery men. My shoulders grew weak until it was a bother to lift my arms, and before I knew it, I wasn't raising my hands even to the height of the doorknob. Staying in was easy enough. I had residuals coming in from a corporate training video I'd done in college. I was living in a house my grandfather had left me when he passed away. My sister showed up every other week to convince her limbs around me and eye my scalp oil, unable to tell me to shower. I'd smile and tell her I was fine. "I'm happy!" I'd say and she'd gather the dirty dishes piled on every surface and heave them into the sink before donning her rubber gloves to scrub off the scum. I could feel cavities nesting in my teeth; I knew the root of one tooth was dead. The pain rang and pounded like someone wanting to be let in. I spoke pulverized truths to my sister trying to get her to relax. "I can leave whenever I feel like it" and "I just need a few minutes to be myself." She'd give up and leave and I'd trace paused cartoons off the screen of my television for fun. The arrangement felt logical at the time.

I refused to admit my behavior was not normal. The outside world and I were like cracked magnets. We had been one and the same, but we'd broken apart and could now do nothing but resist. Every time I considered leaving my home, I wondered what could be waiting for me out there and never came up with an attractive enough answer. It wasn't even fear. That's what I kept telling myself.

I'd sit on my couch and try to catch the sunlight on my watch face. I'd direct the light onto my cat until she chased the slow burn of the reflection. Bugs showed up, cinching themselves through the pipes and the baseboards. My sister would appear to ask me lists of questions out of pamphlets she got at the doctor's office. I'd test myself by trying to guess how she was diagnosing me by the questions she asked. My record was guessing bipolar from the first question. "'I feel so restless or find it so hard to keep still that other people have pointed this out to me.' Do you feel this way 'Rarely,' 'Occasionally,' or 'Most of the Time'?" I said, "Penny, do I look restless? I'm not bipolar," and she stared at me like I had pressed her into some impossible place.

When our mother died back in Tulsa later that year, I wanted to pay my respects. I booked a flight and called a cab. When I walked out my front door, *there* was the proof that that agoraphobia pamphlet didn't apply. I got on a plane and tried to take the stains out of the memories of my mother. The asshole next to me kept forcing his elbows down on the armrest that my hip meat kept forcing up. Eventually he spilled a mess of words into the air at me and moved to sit across the aisle next to a child flying alone. I adjusted that armrest up and relaxed comfortably for the rest of the flight.

I examined the photos my mother had framed all along the staircase: so many of me making smiles like I was dying with forced charm before a dance recital, photos that were sixty percent ceiling, where I clutched bouquets of flowers after the high school musical. I recognized a lingering pride in my belly, and in the reflected glass of the frames, I saw an abstract smile pulling itself from my lips. I had had such hopes, but now when I thought about my ambition, I felt pity. My dream had been to excel at convincing people I was someone else. The intention felt so specific now. It felt sad and misguided. It felt better not to know what the hell I was doing than to think about where that impulse had come from at such a young age.

I thought of the bugs roaming the house back in California and how it felt good to recognize a problem.

I held it together most of that day, meeting with the undertaker and going to the florist with my sister and her family. Not until I went out to the garden and saw one of my mother's footprints still stamped into the waterlogged mud of a flower bed did I cry. My mother had just had the yard resodded. She didn't think she was about to die. You could see the seams stashed all over the lawn where sheet of grass met sheet of grass. I found a single weed that had wormed through the newly laid mess. "It's okay," I thought. "She would have found you." And my mother would have. She was ruthless, determined to a fault. She kept after something until she forgot why she was after it. My mother thrilled every time I got another role, every time I became another option. She seemed sure I'd find someone better to be.

That night in the shower, so much of my hair washed down the drain that I worried I might disappear, but when I wiped off the fogged-up mirror, I saw my head was still full of locks and tangles. I combed it carefully and emerged in pajamas to find my brother-in-law waiting to brush his teeth. "Don't bother," I said. "Come with me." His face lifted slowly and he followed me down the stairs. My sister was at the counter, flipping through my mother's address book, making sure we hadn't missed letting anyone know. I pulled a bottle of rye from under the counter. Surely no one had touched it since my father had passed away. I poured for all three of us and asked my sister who she thought she'd been in our mother's eyes, and who she'd wanted to be. My sister said she'd never thought of it that way, and I said, "Let's."

Half

As often is the case, the situation was nearly impossible to recognize as an ending. Each tried to rehash the circumstances again and again to his or her own advantage. When even every unintended chance had been given to and misused by Benji and Pippa, they knew it must be over. When they were able to see it, when the sunlight finally hit the surface of it in a way that they recognized the crack for what it was, the decision was clean and obvious and certainly a relief. For so long they had both been sure of each other, they knew this break had to be even and sharp in a way that no one could get sentimental or nostalgic.

They owned a good deal of stuff. Neither could recall who purchased what, so lost in each other had they once been, but suddenly King Solomon was remembered by Pippa, and Benji concurred that everything needed to be destroyed. It would be the only way—break it all down and hurl it into large dumpsters.

Cutting tools were purchased by Benji—this was clear—*Benji now owned the destruction equipment.* Diagonal slashes were dragged through every object. They started at the sternum of their home, tearing through books with thick scissor blades. The large chainsaw broke through the center of the couch easily, sending cotton and carcinogenic foam rubber into the air. Pippa went back to the hardware store and purchased bird flu masks. Benji refused one at first, but Pippa expressed her concern—she didn't want the guilt of his slow death to rest on the end of this relationship. He accepted and then perspiration grew around their mouths in equally salty increments.

Pippa sat looking at a necklace Benji had given her and suddenly, metal to metal, wire cutters severed the links into two strands. "Everything," Benji said. Anger and agreement drove Pippa's hands into the shoebox beside her and pulled up a stack of photos, her fingers destroying them in one clean pull of corner from corner. Benji smiled at her, but Pippa couldn't see it under the paper mask. Benji used the CutCo knives to saw through cans of soup and then bent the knives until the blades snapped. Pippa tore through every precious dress she'd sniffed out in thrift stores and sample sales. Benji unplugged the TV before trying the saw on it first and then resorting to the sledgehammer. He didn't pause as he slid each baseball card out of its plastic sheet. Pippa kicked through framed drawings she'd made of Benji. Let's be clear: they meant every word.

When everything had been clipped and ripped and unhinged, Pippa took Benji's hand and hauled him outside. She pushed a shovel into his grip and took one for herself. She pointed to the northwest corner of the yard and she took the southeast. They began digging a diagonal trench through the garden, ruining a full lawn that had taken years to even out because of the heavy shade. It was a generous break from the particulate air of the indoors. Pippa tore off her white mask and Benji did the same.

Questions quickly entered each of their minds, but they replaced them with the work of calculating exactly how many more minutes would pass before this epoch would end. Only several feet of space kept them from the moment they would meet in the center of the yard and spade would clang against spade. They both knew the real work of this decision would come with phone calls and cups of coffee and the hard task of making others understand. Small pools of pity and misunderstanding and alliance would gather between family and friends. Pippa and Benji had only small pockets of fear: elegance, rationality, indecency, skepticism, and forgiveness.

Above them, in a tree, large now but once so small one or the other of them (who could remember?) had been able to carry it with a single hand, a crow sat cawing and searching the branches for life.

With just inches between them, Benji dug in one more time and Pippa met his effort. Breathing hard, perspiration everywhere, they looked behind them at the line that had been drawn and one final thought arrived to their minds at the same time: there is no specified distance between being alone and around.

Judgment Day

When Pewit was a child, his parents told her about the wild Scissortail monster who would decide what her afterlife would be. Pewit had been poring over the Roman heroes of her mother's heritage and the Greek monsters of his father's. Pewit imagined himself away from her parents, in the world of these myths, where things were always and never what they seemed. Pewit's parents saw the way he believed everything was possible and made up a new monster, one that Pewit had not already read about, one that Pewit might think still existed, one that had not yet been conquered by a myth and a hero. They told Pewit about its barbed-wire limbs and its chalk-white nipples. Pewit lived in fear of the Scissortail Beast for a long time, imagined the way it would divide him, the way the Scissortail, with a few quick cuts, could make Pewit one thing, rather than another. How the Scissortail could take away Pewit's bothness. Pewit was tired of only being something when compared to another. Pewit wanted to be the same thing no matter what she was standing next to. Pewit wanted to untitle himself. One afternoon Pewit found a duck in the barn tangled in some unwound fencing wire, dead from fright or exhaustion. On the wall above the duck was a drawing of the Scissortail, just as Pewit had imagined it—its arms raised menacingly. The image of the Scissortail lorded over this trapped dead duck. Pewit was not afraid, though. Pewit had known someone had been crawling into his imagination for weeks now. She looked behind her to see if that person was watching her. Pewit knew if he thought his own thoughts, he would come out fine. Pewit didn't have it figured out but liked it that way. Pewit had been snagging on herself. He had confusions that were more certain than he would admit. Pewit was not one or the other. Pewit would not die and go to just one place. Pewit knew she would be everywhere at once and that the white noise of feeling every sensation at one time would make it feel like she was nowhere at all, and that would feel like home. Pewit pitied the Scissortail for its one-sidedness. The Scissortail had been an invention to make Pewit behave. To show how well he knew what was the right thing to do, Pewit reached his small arms carefully into the barbed wire and extracted the duck, cautious not to puncture its unfeeling body but scarring himself. Pewit brought it into her mother to pre-pare for dinner. Then Pewit walked calmly to the bathroom, lined up the antiseptic, the band-aids and his arms, and did the careful work of making sure every bit of herself remained intact.

Hammer, Damper

Before they took him in, he'd made a ritual of pressing his ear to the side of the upright piano as his mother played until she'd warn him away.

Now, in the dark of the night, lit with red blinks and glowing screens and the light from the hall, he watches his parents sleep in the chair and the cot beside him, and he is not old enough to think, "How serious could it be?" He waves his hands, trying to vanish them like he saw in the magic show. He imagines walking out of this place on a tightrope and emerging on the other side of the wall to much applause. When the sun appears in his window at five a.m., he flourishes his palms again. He wonders at how fine he feels.

The father falls for the dark wood laminate, telling people it's a fine room they're living out of these days. The child tinkers with the blood in the tubing when his parents are preoccupied with the doctor. He can make the deep red stop and start with just a pinch. His imagination shapes itself based on his surroundings; he dreams himself a nurse, a doctor. Even when he imagines blaring on a trumpet, he is holding the nebulizer, blowing sour notes sweet. His IV becomes the ripcord on this parachute as he envisions telling his coach, "Maybe we should turn back," before jumping toward the center of the earth. His childhood is possessed by this place. Tangles of days swirl back and forth and none of the family can recognize the present, but they resolve to smile: sad smiles and weary smiles and mesmerized smiles when the doctor brings news that says, "Improvement has come in the form of staying the same."

Each night abounds with the invisible impossible. What if the child fell from bed and none of the alarms laughed their cruel laugh? The parents bring in a radio to keep the child's ears filled with the same piano mazurkas and polkas he loved, but the child misses the vibrations, the small violences of the hammers dancing on the wires just inches from his face.

The parents' wingspans grow smaller. Their car hasn't been touched in days.

"That noisy sun. Tell it to shut up," the boy says in the afternoon, his eyes squinting, and the parents squelch their scolding and close the blinds. They miss the way the light warms their core and mourn the cacophony of life outside the window, but they keep telling themselves, "It is not the skin of *our* teeth."

The child mouths gibberish much of the afternoon, drifting into a kind of stupor, anesthetic shooing or beckoning. The mother reads to the child even after he has fallen asleep: "A fox remembers easily." She pauses on this, stranded.

The children who are well enough put on a play. It takes weeks to prepare. It makes the father's tears ceiling within his eyes each time he thinks of it. The parents take their son to see it, but the play is about a garden, and the garden is just off-stage. It drives the mother into a fit by the end of the show, knowing that off-stage there is no garden at all. She tells the director, "I would have folded colored tissue. I would have pinched together fabric scraps so these children could have had a real garden." Some of the kids overhear her and look around, confused. They do not know what might have been.

Grandmother visits and she is full of laughter and soft to hug. Grandmother gives charming warnings for the future and the parents look away, convinced of what is not to come. They hold the point of view of each visitor in their mouths until it becomes soggy and they spit it out. They have come to vie for the insoluble. They have made up a new way to survive knowing what they know. They no longer hesitate or whisper or experience anticipation. They used to shimmer with restlessness, and now they blink largo.

The father read that animals that breathe more slowly—pythons, elephants, tortoises—live longer. The family begins losing sleep in the attempt to breathe more and more slowly, and so even their breath becomes strange to them. They slow their heart rates by seventy-five percent. They hibernate awake.

The parents read to the child about everything in the hopes of telling him the one thing he needs to know. "Breathing is one of the few things we can both *control* and *not* about our bodies. That means, it happens without our thinking about it, but we can also think about it and change the way it happens."

The child is familiar with things that he can't stop, so he listens carefully.

The father reports, "Conscious breathing is found in many forms of meditation and exercise and performance: yoga, swimming, vocal training, the playing of musical instruments. You can change your unconscious efforts slowly." The mother caresses the back of the child's head and says, "Unconscious breathing starts back here in your brainstem."

The child, trying to wrap around this information, asks, "So I could stop my breath? I could end?"

The parents look at each other nervously, want to run to another room and punch the other's lights out for thinking this was a good idea. Instead they silently agree what a privilege it is to live so closely to this pocket of wonder they call their son.

The father says, "No. A person cannot just voluntarily stop breathing. Your reflexes would cause you to breathe or you would lose consciousness and your body would breathe for you."

The mother changes the subject quickly. "Hippocrates thought you could determine a person's health by their breath."

When the doctor comes in with his brain full of news and his mouth full of reassurance, the child begins to cry and his color begins to change, but no one notices, for they're all torn apart by the prognosis. The child falls off into a forced sleep, the pain having stopped his breath. The parents weep all the more loudly, so they don't notice one missing voice, one absent pattern of inhales and exhales. The doctor notices the child's color only after he has already stranded himself in a faint.

The doctor uses complex words there are easier translations for: cyanosis, syncope, hypoxia, postictal. There is so much that the child's body needs energy for, but not this education.

The child awakes an hour later with more tears. He can remember all of it. He wishes for forgetting. He asks them to turn the sun away.

When they all fall down into sleep again, the nurses arrive in fleets, carefully watching over the family, keeping the hushed, unspoken ritual of vigilance. The elders wake before the child, feeling negligent and whispering their wishes for rescue as if hidden by dark branches.

The flame of the child is dying out. Words spread quickly as they make their way down to the valley of the cafeteria. The parents torch themselves with coffee, uttering on the view from every window. The mother hisses and spits, and with time they begin to compose themselves with the tenderness necessary to return to the child. They hike back up the floors, calibrating their proximity.

Above the gentle breeze of monitors and ventilation comes a knock at the door, almost impossible to hear. And again, topsy-turvy news. And again, the mother misunderstanding herself. And again, the contemplation of their little stamp of outside world beyond the glass of this awful place. And again, new arrivals of cheery flowers. But the summoning happens all too quickly. What little potential they thought was theirs is rioting.

The loud will soon perish for the quiet. The mother will croon out the happiest songs, transubstantiated to doleful lullabies. She will think of the nest she's formed in the left ventricle of her heart just for the child. The child will grow lighter than an inflatable beach ball. The mother will squeeze him to her chest, afraid he might be carried away.

"There is time for one more story," she tells him, and she squeezes herself on the bed beside him as the child drifts away in the current. In his dream, a voice tells the child to be wary of walking down the chalk path for fear of brushing it away. "Like breadcrumbs," says the voice. "Be fearful of erasure." The child refuses the fear and leans into the wind. A glowing magnificence, he reflects everything. The sun cups him so pointedly that even his eyelids don't hide the light. Those around him can hear his breath curving in coils of alarm, but the child has been rendered graceful.

As people get older, their lives pass at an ever-dizzying pace. People close themselves off with certainty. People laugh less and less. But when death snarls so close and hungry behind a young child, the child, in all his slow-motion time and openness, might invite the wolf in. There is room for new kinds of friendship and new shapes for hope.

For everyone else, the end is full of fervor and calamity. The parents try to flex reality. They try to stretch life a little longer, like the moon in the morning. But then pressure. But then sitting down to play a piano with keys arranged backwards. Impossible anger. Radiant denial. Resounding disorder. Time will teach the way, but first everything will have to be unlearned. The hammers will hug the strings; the strings will shake free.

Unaccounted

Pochard's eyes buckle with the sight of scratches in the wall like bent nails. Bent nails covering the floor like broken fingers. What Pochard needs is a dead pulse. What Pochard says sounds the right way.

Pochard waits with a camera hung round his neck, can feel the hard streaks on the side of his face left behind by a slap, the spin and drag of being watched. What he wanted was the shame of alarms sounding, the orgasm of suggestion. Pochard wanted to feel trapped, like the tight water of a still lake. He wanted to feel pulled firm, like the snap of a snakeskin belt. Instead, he felt full of half-light and the patience of waiting for the right time to speak up.

"Tell me later," his lover would say. "Shallow and easy." But he knew he had been let go when he came upon the simple scene he did. She had dented their connection. In this small house that crouched on a block of mansions, his life had been sold out from under him. His mind was loose with mothers and thieves, either offering useless advice or clearing him out.

He could think of only his lover's knobby teeth, shining broad through her smile now. He thought of children and powder kegs. He was hungry, but steered and muttered that feeling away.

He thought of when they'd met in the church hall, of the way her hips had hauled and bossed their way over to him.

Of how they mixed their glances and how the Savior careened and sloped in his mind, trying to get him back on track. He had breathed in the scent of her and thought of burning candles and handfuls of pennies. He repeated her unusual name in his head: Grebe, Grebe, Grebe. Like the firm beeps of a heart monitor.

He avoided cracks in the sidewalk on his way home, like he believed again. He was thirty-eight, and he'd almost given up. He thought of her fluid wrists, which had curled like ribbon against scissor blades. His face, he was sure, had crawled with surprise as her eyes imploded into their sockets each time she blinked.

Once they had one another, they left the rest behind. They made a ritual of each other. Grebe proved difficult early on and Pochard reveled in it. She lied and cried, and he had dreams of Lady Macbeth. He tried to tune her out. He left sticks inside her mouth as placeholders, spread roads out across her body, eyed the trails of gathering tattoos like a shimmering gas leak, and when that wasn't enough, they found new habits.

Pochard watched the thick slide of tar through Grebe, nauseously conscious of her ruin. He smelled the mesquite cling to her. He gave up his back pockets to her to try and help. He watched her roll into rooms like a truck without brakes. He italicized himself to fit into this new lifestyle; he pulled himself sideways. He dropped a mess of postcards across the country, trying to make sure someone always knew where to find him, if he needed looking for.

He scrubbed her stains and nudity and filth. He fell into and crawled out of that space between too many times to keep blaming her for it. He made temples and rubbed sharp corners round.

But still he wanted her fist in his mouth. He wanted to feel the cotton of her skin magnet to him with sweat. He wanted to taste the metal of her blood and feel the gold flecks of her eyes shine all fake on him. He wanted one more dark summer. He wanted to feel one more wall close in. The tiny electric motors in him began telling the truth, but he ignored them.

Now, after the months they'd spent together, after she'd turned out to be the one to swat him away, he wondered at how clocks must have pocketed the time away, at how he'd never learned his lesson, at how the fear boated through the murk of *him*, rocking and sinful. The windows bundled the light in and made it all clear.

The Crickets Try to Organize Themselves Into Some Raucous Pentameter

A gulch split Odette down the middle and she had the world believing this was the way she liked it. Odette spent entire days bending backward within herself, never letting on that she was uncomfortable, out of her element, ready to leave.

Odette had fallen in love with a waitress who was too good to be true. Odette thought the woman looked familiar and asked if they'd met somewhere. The waitress said, "Nope. I remember everyone I haven't met." Odette tried again the next weekend, made sure she was seated at an appropriate table. Nothing.

Odette dreamed of the waitress, dreamed she found a red silk blouse on the ground in the woods, and several yards up, she found the shirtless waitress crouched in a bush. Odette dreamed she handed the waitress her blouse with her head turned and then the waitress walked out of the woods while Odette walked farther in. The dream happened again and again. Odette went to the restaurant the next week. Still nothing.

The next time she had the dream she crossed a shallow brook before she found the red blouse in the woods, and when she found the waitress in the bush, after she'd put her blouse back on, the waitress said, "The water is taught to become wider." Then the waitress walked back, and when Odette followed her several minutes later, the waitress was almost to the clearing, a full stretch of rapid river between them.

Odette returned to the restaurant and the waitress said, "Listen, I will never remember you, okay? I have been yumped up too many times and I'm not ready for it to happen again." That killed Odette. She left a bigger tip that night.

Odette returned to the restaurant the next week and the waitress said, "Listen, you act like you know what I'm doing, but you don't. Trust me."

Odette said, "All I've got is every minute of the day."

The next week, she went for a drink at the 400 Club instead. She felt uncomfortable in low-class places, like she was pretending. All these people saying they preferred a dump, but she required a bartender in a collared shirt, a clean glass, a hand-stuffed olive. She couldn't help but feel the money within her. At the 400 Club, a banker appreciated her youth, thought she was an escort. "I'd like to use your dress as an alibi, if it's all right with you." She accepted the drink he offered her and hoped the mirrors would carry her off into some netherworld while he went on. Before long, his thumb bones cocked up and down her knee and she would be lying if she said she didn't enjoy it.

The banker asked Odette if he could lure her home with him for a nightcap. Odette said, "You'll have to delay the sunrise if you want *me* to go anywhere with *you*." She'd drunk enough to arrange herself into poems that he wouldn't understand. He urged her on, unable to take a circuitous "no" for an answer, but she spouted off another refusal: "I'm sure you've got a lot of spare change and guts in your piggy bank, but I'm going to my own home alone before the light reveals me."

"Odette is the world is Odette."

The banker pouted. "Can I get your number?"

Odette shook her pretty little head. "You can have my permanence and the rest of *this* rotgut." She handed him her glass and he drained it. There were enough napkins on the bar, but the banker pulled a fountain pen from his jacket pocket and wrote his number on Odette's arm.

She watched the runny ink bleed between her skin cells. By the time she got home it would be unreadable. "Classy," she slurred.

Odette did nothing that week. She thought, "I wish that asshole would have written his number on a goddamn napkin." When the next weekend rolled around she went back to the 400 Club, the banker already at the bar, talking to another girl. Odette walked up to him anyway.

The banker frowned at her. "You didn't call me." He looked over at his new companion as if to say, "So this is what has happened."

Odette said, "The ruins were profound and formful, but totally unreadable."

The banker nodded. "Nice to see you though."

Odette walked away; some sentiments she understood.

She drank her whiskeys slowly and alone, eavesdropping for a while on a bottle blonde ranting at her companion about how they never went out for nice dinners anymore. She listened to more of the conversation and built her remaining suspicions carefully. This woman had found her meal ticket in a guy who was tall, well-built, attractive, but obviously lacked confidence for one reason or another. This man could do better than a bleach job with a hunger for fancy dinners and an allowance.

Odette spun on her stool to get a look at the man over the shoulder of the blonde, and before too long the man couldn't hide his attentions and both he and his companion had turned to Odette.

"Can I help you with something?" the blonde asked Odette.

"Put your mask back on, sweetie." Odette was ready for a fight.

The blonde said, "Excuse me?"

Odette shrugged and looked over to the blonde's companion, raising her eyebrows. He smiled a little and then tried to take it back. The blonde kept looking back and forth between them, until she was disoriented and her anger carried her off.

"I needed that," the man told Odette. "You saved me."

Odette offered her arm. "Take me for a walk."

The man was anxious not to lose his chance. "It's raining out there, you know."

"We'll admire the light catching the umbrellas together." The man looked a little stunned. He didn't know the game of saying extraordinary things, but Odette thought, "I'll teach him."

This man was an engineer who didn't engineer anymore. They strolled the wet streets and he began talking about how it was tomorrow already and how tomorrow, today, marked the anniversary of the bomb being dropped on Hiroshima.

Odette thought, "This guy has a long way to go," and so she said one of her extraordinary things. "Can you imagine the bodies trying to heal themselves? The contrast of their wet new skin to the cremains around them? The pattern of a dress burnt onto a woman in patches?"

The engineer who no longer engineered looked at her with the boned vision of envy and disgust. The engineer would not play the game and so Odette said she was heading home. He asked if he could give her a ride, but Odette refused and walked the miles carefully in her heels, hesitating and imaginative.

Odette returned to the restaurant to see the waitress the next night.

The waitress remembered her. "What is it you want from me?" the waitress asked.

Odette started, "Well, I believe in a slanted precision to all things..."

"No," the waitress said. "What's your order?"

Odette sighed. She ordered and said nothing as each course was delivered to her. Odette sat, eating and remembering how she sometimes forgot to pretend romance into situations. She thought about how she needed to stop the self-conscious bullshit and buy into a grand gesture or two.

The waitress returned, and Odette caught her arm. "I've spilled so many sing-alongs of what I knew I was supposed to say. I'm not doing that here." Odette saw the startle turn to tears and knew her time was limited, so she played every card. "I've tried talking to other people, and you confuse me best. I want my memories to meet yours. I want to collapse beneath your complexities. I want to feel a million small surgeries knit us together. I don't want to let myself down and I don't want to avoid the hardest options. Come have a drink with me when your shift ends."

The waitress lied and told the truth and said, "Yes," figuring she'd change her mind later.

At the end of the night the waitress didn't know where Odette had gone, and so she packed up and headed out. Odette sat smiling on a bench a couple blocks down "With so many events and so many memories, it's easy to forget which is which."

The waitress took Odette's proffered arm and they headed down the street to the 400 Club, where she apologized for not being dressed right. Odette said, "Get serious. Your face dresses you up." Odette could tell the waitress was impressed, and then Odette wondered if she wanted a woman who could be impressed by this schmaltz.

The banker was alone, down the bar. He wandered closer and grinned, all sly and circular, at Odette and the waitress. "Didn't I saw you in half once?" he asked and Odette turned to the waitress and shook her head. "What's your friend's name?"

Odette didn't know her name, so she kept quiet. This problem was out of her hands, but Odette hoped it would grow less familiar. Odette looked into the waitress's eyes and her wish came true: the waitress brought her lips right up to Odette's ear and whispered her name, so only she would hear: *Farrah.* Odette was over the moon; she loved this name so much. She turned to the banker, and said, "This one's mine," and the banker took "no" for an answer.

Farrah began telling stories but never looked Odette in the eye. Closing time snuck up on them and they would need to exit into the hurrying air. Odette said nothing, just listened to Farrah tell it. Odette tuned in and out as she stared at this lovely girl: "My knife digs into apple upon apple...This god who had recently named his rivals...Three sisters sit in a dark room as their father walks through unaware of their presence and when he is out of earshot, they slap hands...Cicadas emerge like specters." Here was a girl who knew the game without naming it.

Odette dropped Farrah at her apartment, kissed her cheek. "The things we say can crystallize our future in many ways." And with that, Odette climbed back in the cab and Farrah remained standing on the stoop, trying to remember all of the things she'd said.

In the cab, sleep had made a fist of itself, and Odette was unsure she would make it the long ride home without being knocked out. But by the time the driver pulled up to her building she had caught a second wind and was laughing giddily at the unavoidability of death and taxis.

She didn't fall into her bed, but instead filled her bathtub with water and clipped strand after strand of pearls until every pearl she owned rested on the bottom of the tub. She dunked her head underwater and rescued each pearl, sucking it into her mouth and then spitting it onto the fluffy bath mat. She experienced an abstract panic many times as she lost a pearl and found it again.

She trawled the bottom of the tub with her soft lips. Coming up empty, she found she'd rescued each pearl. She scooped the pearls into a soap dish, her lungs tired and her neck aching from the angles. She shed her clothes, loosened her body onto her big bed, and slept—mute, dreamless.

A Heaven Gone

Misery is an awful kinship. Windows of humor roll down low and whistle at our glorious legs and gawk at the stiff and enthronging death of accidents. The humpbacked light of the moon is the funnel cloud of direction, sawn off and mighty. We smoke bouquets of tobacco and flex our thumbs like whales surfacing through the sunny thickness of the air. The bright edge of the sea is half a country away and we are dry and walking through muddy woodsmoke curtains that call themselves the great wide open. We drape our emptiness on the spiky pickets along the way, old plastic bags we've no use for. At night the caliginous demons of shadowy ditches beside us are full or not, and the violence of air passing us behind vehicles is cozy and cool. We watch some sort of bird fly up the sky in a frenzy and analyze the constellations of oak trees out at the edge of that field. We are a heaven gone from where we came from now and the filth of myths covers most of this journey. I am growing

fat even now beneath this hunger and I am
sorry. The humble pair of us just needs a
ride to the other ocean, free of bullets and
wrinkles. One of us is sure to die feeling
all of this. We load our possessions into
a truck and close our hands around them
again too soon to throw them down to the
dusty ground again. I start to think things
are blowing up around me when nothing
is happening, in entire moments of quiet.
I descend even myself and lose hope but
then there are pauses where I discover it
again and this hope vamps until it becomes
arrhythmic again and I lose the beat and
the melody. Then it's just the same used
silences to try to fill me up. Our conversations resort to double entendres and
factoids, and our imaginations begin to
travel that impossible and outward journey where even we don't know how long
it's been that the sun has been high or
that a car hasn't passed. Our consolation
is that even dry land creates horizons and
we are always standing at someone else's.
Our showy outsides, old and dirty as they
are, lie and say there's a jingling being
right beneath all that dust. It keeps raining
all the time for a while and then not. We
find a barn and are tempted by it, but not
enough. We imagine the horse in the middle of it, silhouetted by the slatted walls.
We stop thinking and rely on the fossiliza-
tion of opinions we made long ago. Our

attraction to each other changes or at least wanders. We drink whiskey in a cab with a fragrant lion of a man. We try a train but those are filled with sorrows and stories of women. We feel certain of something and then it repeats itself so we lose certainty. We take it all too seriously and then don't care. After it'd happened, they told us, "It will take time to heal, take a long walk home." A factory of road rolls somewhere out of sight before us and creates the tarred surfaces for our feet to move upon. Some days, the way the ground moves, the distance we've traveled feels more like the zigzag of beads on an abacus than an arrow. We feel much like tumbleweeds rolling until a truck sweeps us up and pitches us out again. We examine each reliquary dashboard with its beliefs and statues. Estranged youth: that is what we are called again. People ask what we're estranging ourselves from and we say spirits and rivers and hectic, exotic pistols and childhood and jobs and crime, just to keep it exciting. In each cab we shoulder ignorance and we keep our mouths shut when we can. When we can't we descend the thickets of weeds beside the shoulder. We dance at the bulges of cannonball thunder. We don't talk about it when the rain doesn't come. "Gotta be kidding," we say again and again. Occasionally nickels and dimes slap the ground at our feet. We flap around trying to gather the coins. It's too many degrees, but we're getting close. It is not beautiful. We are listening less and less. Birds of paper blow by again and again. Then, finally: a bay. Our feet travel us onto the solid land of a deck. Backwards like the lee of encouragement the water passes smears of history and the clustering eyeballs. Unrecoverable flotsam in the paint and thin ropes of bridges make up most of my collection. There is nothing solid out here but that on which we stand. We have barely begun, but already we are left alone by the land.

Like Lightning

Jenny, with her wasp waist and breath like stinging lemons. Jenny's husband is very ill. Full, alienated clauses of time are being pulled through IVs, sucked into his life-thirsty body. Jenny thinks, "Maybe my mid-gut will quit before his," and quickly stops her thoughts.

Six children bang the ground around her. Six children who have emerged from her thorax: newfangled, right-handed. Six glorious exits that became entrances.

The swinging fraudulence of "forever" brushes the side of her face again and again and again, rubbing it raw. She is surrounded, albeit alone, with six beehive minds, quick to omit the worst facts.

Friends travel into his room to make blank truces, last-ditch efforts to make indelible marks on him.

Jenny's eyes, full of so many angles, sense the world framing these instants for her memory. She is compelled to doubt almost everything. She often misses the point. Some foreign filmmaker's mind is converting everything to images.

Summer is spent in a carefully air-conditioned laboratory of a room.

Time quickens. The silt of everyday encounters adds up to more. Six weeks drop away, leave Jenny so tired she doesn't have the energy or space to flap her wings into flight. Her balance is off. She is heavy with the loneliness that awaits.

Then, one day, an anonymous deliveryman arrives with cases of an expected yet unknown substance. As her husband turns back to make sure she follows him, his breath halts. Simple marching songs play in the air. She doesn't care to concern herself with the truth. Not even a single question presents itself. This moment has been living within her for months.

This darkness cradles the room until the light of six unborn stars bursts in to shine full sentences of future upon her.

Before We Pass This Way Again

The final sight of him almost went unnoticed. She might have said "Thank you" rather than "Farewell," but by then Louie knew her own mind. She recognized the sound of him leaving for what it was.

When it came down to just the two of them, they went to McDonald's almost every day. Louie got good at faking what a treat it was. Her father'd flip in the Townes van Zandt tape as they pulled out of the driveway. He knew the importance of consistency. To Louie, this meant they'd known each other a long time. Louie even silently picked them a song—"Be Here to Love Me Today." When the first chords of this song sounded, her father's hand always went to the volume knob, twisted it clockwise. They both sang along. Louie's father got a word wrong, mistook one verse for another, and hummed the rest of the line like he meant it.

Him eating a Big Mac, her chicken nuggets, he gave her advice, probably because he didn't know what else to do. Most of the time it was completely unrelated to the trials of growing up appropriate to Louie's age: "Never be grateful to a boy. He's benefiting from the deal, and if you play it right, he'll be grateful for whatever attention you give him. He's the one should be grateful to you." Louie nodded her head solemnly, unblinking. She didn't like to talk to boys. She didn't want to ask what deal her father was talking about.

With her father, she didn't go to church on Sundays anymore. They slept late and they headed out to the cemetery first thing. Louie kicked freshly cut grass from the headstone and it clung to her patent leather shoes. "Why do women die?" she asked her father. He shook his head like he missed her mother too. After a moment, he'd take her hand and lead her back to the truck. They drove in silence to the bar. That was just the way he did things: cheap fast food to eat and top-shelf liquor for drinking.

"Do you remember your mama?" he asked as he pulled out the bar stool for her. Louie wished he'd asked at the cemetery. At her mother's grave, her head had been clear with grass and sunshine; here she felt dizzy with the yeasty smell of old beer and the ammonia they used to try to scrub it away. She answered, though, because he hardly ever asked about her mama. "Of course. It hasn't even been a year yet, Daddy." Her father nodded at this and then looked down the bar. The bartender headed toward them, stopping to pour a Coke and scoop a dozen cherries into a cocktail glass for Louie. The bartender then looked at her father. "Jack?" was all she said and he nodded. He didn't need to say much because he never really changed.

Her grandparents wanted to see her. It'd been months, they said. They wanted to make sure she was clean and eating well. Really, though, they missed their daughter and wanted to see what remained of her. To ensure the safety of that last little bit. They'd never trusted Louie's father.

He brought Louie out to their farm. The dust from the truck still settling, Louie hopped to the ground and ran to her grandparents.

Why he stuck around was anyone's guess. They all assumed he'd slow down to let Louie out and return to pick her up when she was ready to come on home. It was summer; Louie had nowhere to be. She could stay all season, if she wanted.

After dinner one night her father nudged Louie's knee with his own. "Sing for your grandparents."

She looked up from her cobbler, terrified.

"She's got a real pretty voice." He nodded at his mother- and father-in-law. It was probably the first he'd spoken since they'd arrived. Everyone seemed a little stunned. Louie's grandparents looked at her expectantly because they didn't know how to look at her father.

"Go on, Lou. You know the one I like." He placed his big, rough hand on the table and began to drum it lightly. Right away she knew it was the song she'd claimed as their own. She started crying. Everyone thought it was because she didn't want to sing.

The next morning, her father and grandfather drank coffee on the porch while Louie chased the cat around the yard. Her grandmother sat on a swing that still hung from a branch of the tree out front. She snapped her old Polaroid camera, all of the pictures coming out golden.

The cat ran beneath the porch and Louie fell to the ground, exhausted. Her grandmother called to her, "Come here and sit on my lap, Louise. You'll get your new dress all dirty." She was too big for her grandmother's lap, but Louie went to her anyway. Her grandmother leaned down to lift her and Louie kissed her cheek and escaped behind the swing to push her grandmother's ample behind. "Louise! I'm too heavy!" Louie continued though, and her grandmother laughed at her feeble attempts.

After a walk down the road to visit the horses at the neighbor's stable, the four of them drove into town for lunch. At the diner, Louie examined the menu carefully and asked if she could order spaghetti for lunch. Her grandfather kissed her forehead and said, "Anything you want."

Louie pressed her luck and asked for a milkshake as well.

"With your spaghetti?" her grandmother asked. Louie didn't know how to answer, so she didn't, but her grandfather repeated himself. "Anything you want."

When the waitress came again, Louie ordered and her father said, "I'll have the same."

Everyone looked at him with lifted eyebrows, but no one said a word.

The silence was long after the waitress left. "Sing for your grandparents? Please, Lou?" Her father didn't pose it as a command this time; he asked her.

Louie had stayed up half the night preoccupied with the thought of singing. Now that her father made the request again, she felt that with a little time she could get up the courage to do it. She needed a moment to gather herself and in that moment her grandparents took her silence for fear and began bickering about whose turn it was to sweep the porch once they got back to the farm.

Louie dragged the crayons she was given across the paper tablecloth as she began to hum. Her father's eyes leaned toward what she was drawing: a horse like the silver one she'd seen that afternoon. Soon the humming formed into words, like her father's botched lyrics rewound. She sang their song slowly and mournfully. She was already to the second verse when her grandmother hushed her grandfather and nodded to Louie, who continued to draw as her voice grew. She knew she had their attention, but she thought if she looked up the fear might erase her voice. Her father watched her hands. Louie's voice was soft, too small to silence a room, but it filled their booth and spilled over just a little bit to the tables beside. She finished like it was nothing. Her grandparents' eyes brimmed. Their food arrived and everyone ate in silence.

It was Louie's father who finally spoke, after their plates were cleared. He lit a cigarette. "If I might take the liberty to say it, your Chandra's voice bent around corners better'n any slide guitar's song. I remember one afternoon when she was pregnant with Lou, we were sittin' in our kitchen and she started hummin', soft, all edges she kept tight to.

"Through the window, her voice carried. We'd raised the storm glass so the breeze could skate in underneath. We sat at the table, drops of water gathering on our juice glasses.

"I remember she was singin' 'bout stallions, but it was that voice that galloped at the first thunder crack. The rain started slow, sped up as her song did.

"Sometimes I wasn't sure the sounds she was makin' anyone else'd call singin'. It was more like talkin', but there was this clarity to it that made me cool all over.

"I don't know where she found those words. She'd come to me to learn earlier that year: saddles, bridles, gaits. She wanted it, so she learned quick. Now she was singin' of the horses like she'd been born to'm.

"I was afraid to move. I didn't want to spook'er into silence. The sound was risin' out of her like heat. The rain was pourin', bouncin' off the windowsill onto our bare arms.

"Her body was heavy then and as she sang she grew more and more relaxed. Her legs splayed around Lou, still inside of her and 'bout ready to come out. Her shoulders dropped. Only her head shook ever so slowly as those notes came out.

"And I remember, all of a sudden, I just couldn't take it. I couldn't take how she could make me change just like that. Right away, I just got so sad and I told her to stop. Her eyes opened after her voice quit. She didn't ask any questions. We just sat and listened to what was left."

They were all quiet for a long time again. Everyone sipped their coffee.

"I think I need to leave Lou here with you for a while."

Louie looked up at her father. She'd known as soon as he started talking about her mama, it wouldn't be long. He could never stick around after he started thinking about her. Even if he stayed in the same place, he checked out until he knew her memory had cleared. Her grandparents nodded. Louie could tell they were torn. They were happy to have the last little bit of their daughter, but they were also thinking, "We were right; we knew he couldn't handle her." Everyone gathered their belongings and headed to the street. Louie and her grandmother walked slowly, peeking into shop windows. Her father and grandfather walked ahead a ways, talking quietly. While she looked at a dollhouse, full of its tiny perfections, she heard an engine start and looked back to see her father pull away. Neither waved. Louie certainly didn't cry.

Her grandmother took her hand. "What do you say we walk on home?"

Louie nodded.

On that last day, on the long walk back to the farmhouse, she wondered if it wasn't just the fact that she was made out of a lot of mind and he was a lot of world. She hummed a little as she scuffed her shoes, kicking rocks. She thought about how much more quickly she could move with a horse beneath her; she wondered when she would get to learn.

The Chamber of the Enigma

"You tell me," Buzzard whispers in my ear. Buzzard and I made a baby, but that baby ain't anything like we'd ever expected. Think of a doll the size of a boy. Think of a mannequin plucked from the children's section: vague and featureless. Buzzard and I are small and soft, malleable and hand-powered. Where had this blank and stiff being come from?

"Buzzard," I say, "you better pony up the cash to get this boy to the doctor. I don't know how to care for a thing like this."

Buzzard's eyes sweat rhinestones as he stares at me. "We'll love him," Buzzard says, raising his hand and gesturing to the boy, making a toast to the con man of his sadness.

"Snap out of it, Buzzard!" I say. "I'm gonna need your help here. You can't be glazed and spilling for all eternity. You can't let your head circle round and round. You gotta land." I slap him hard and he finally focuses.

The doll-child is hard to read—he makes no sound and moves not a muscle. It is hard to know if the doll-child is even alive. If he is living, he is an invalid, and he must be lonely inside himself.

Buzzard stutters around the room, watching the doll-child. I sneer and chase my own tail, trying to think what to do. I swaddle the doll-child in several of my tulle dresses. The child is already at least three times my size. I'm starving, but my needs aren't the thing to think of anymore.

I look at Buzzard, but he's not looking at anything. Then I look at the doll-child and think, "The first thing we'll need is something to call him by." He has a head of fine black hair all curling around itself. I look deep into the child's eyes and wonder if there's anything in them. I wonder where the key is to this iron box. I wonder when everything that he's made of will well up and surprise us all. Finally, I say his name like I'm saying "thank you."

Things don't get easier. We call the doll-child Bluebird. When I try to talk to him, my mouth tangles like rosebushes. The thickness of my tongue dances slow, like pushing stones. I feel deaf and late. Bluebird lies listless. I never hear him laugh; his focus, control, stillness are constant. Even his breathing is just a measured ripple. I enter his room, burnt and swinging. I trumpet and crumple, trying to get a rise from him. I am collapsing-tired on the sidelines of him. He is daytime television. He is silly profanity. He is a white gardenia that blooms too long, brown on the edges and sweet in an uninvited way.

I ask my mother what I need to do, and she says his needs should attack me like a bear. When I smell him, I change him. I flush with the effort of rolling water and soap down his body. I grow used to the sound of the old sand through the hourglass and his silent refusal to sleep. I read him stories of countesses and counts dressed in rich, blue velvet. My mother visits and stares as she watches me care for him, declining her turn to speak. Buzzard does just what he said he'd do: loves him. And that's about it.

I tell myself over and over that I don't mind all that I give up for Bluebird and wonder, with my weak brain, if the Lord is sarcastic. Bluebird grows bigger, his skin stretches over new bones, the growing pains pulling him beautiful and awkward.

He smiles like an anchorman for a while, and I wonder what's better: his blank slate or this horror.

I try to rouse him, but his fatigue is spotless. I try to drag him through the small knot of the doorway, out into the world. I gasp nervously when people ask about him. I seek advice in private, and everyone has a different thing to say. To let him ghost if that's the stage he's in. To try and light him like a cigarette. To pop my own laughter outside his door to lure him out.

People ask what worries me most, and I say the fear isn't really sorted out that way. I wake and retrieve the pressure I shed in my sleep. I keep checking on him and expecting things of him. My Bluebird, a grumbling stump, his hands hid, his mouth shut, convinced all of this something is a nothing. My eyes jangle, my cheeks dry and show lavish tilts of salt. Every day more and more crashes into the walls. I want to go too far, I want a neon sign to let me know this is worth waiting for.

The Colleens

The Colleens cruise their shadows again along the window-sills, discriminately in the nightshade alone. They peek in. The Colleens, though? You won't see them back. They deviate from any usable light. Their straight golden hair stretches artfully over one eye like an invisibility cloak. A band of pretty girls, unnaturally menacing, becomes unnoticeable. Their fingers spin at their waists like Turing machines. The equation is never solved; the digital dervishes gain speed.

Piloting these Colleens is a gentle North Light, dispatching them like the couriers of some repeatable secret message. Again and again they meet the approach of the night but never recognize the falling of the watery darkness as a stop sign. The calm and legible way the Colleens ride their feet through the evening presents them with the immense time hidden in sleep. Good hour after hour takes them on mental journeys. Every bit of their interiors has been raided, and so they wander like the Burghers of Calais, willing yet not wanting to give themselves for the good of the people. The Colleens want, without pursuing their desire, to wear the hats of others but proceed not able to recognize anything beyond the pattern of steps they take.

The Colleens shepherd the night into each small town, and when it is safe, when a sufficient amount of time has passed, the light will brutalize familiar streets again.

Engrossed

We is preoccupied and headless. We takes the open invitation of mirrors and stares without eyes and the pressure thins to a prop. We wheels the piano into sun showers and watches the warp and hustle. We pains and flashes with strange gestures. We cannot be love that works. That suicide be stopping in a residual and curtsying way: it are cute like thumbs and nipples and unexpected swelling. We bites your will like a ball of wool. Your body flood us and we rocks and fogs, delivering. The climate outside our body are a busy woman. We takes a nap every hundred feet. The silence realizes again and we is water-hungry. We drinks our brothers and the frame are everything we can't forgive, driving and tricky. We likes your language with exceptions. We clicks and zippers through this light rain. You can memorize our mind in one go. We kittens down empty roads like old winter. There is floods and glass eyes and nothing that resembles what you knows to look for in the middle of the day. We cushions your head, delicate and crested. Desire wills itself through muscle and moist dreams dusts our arteries. We started out less human than this. Our lips was pink and amphibian. No bruise is as real as the one wrought by the engine in our chest. Ruthless green interruptions truth my starving blood. Instead of "we am," say "we will."

The Direction of Forgetting

To travel the incense road requires a man to lay down his longing in favor of the will for adventure and wealth. He must put aside the scents of his lover and let the turmeric grow comfortable deep in his lungs, easy as breath. One must prepare to find threads of saffron clinging to his cloak and pluck them thoughtfully away, as if they were strands of his wife's golden hair.

In Java I lose the details of my wife's skin when I plunge my hands deep into a sack of weaver bird feathers. I trade, with a plastered urgency, a surplus of cinnamon we'd been carting since Aden for the sack of plumage.

That night, in my inner cabin room, I examine one of the bright quills carefully, stroking it against the grain, and wedge it into the band of my hat. A shipmate summons me with a bald knocking—the rats have cracked a barrel of wormwood and are stumbling about the hold. They've become emboldened, are approaching deck hands with curious noses and mouths. I go to examine the ravaged barrel, slats splayed out like so many petals of some stiff flower, and find a quiet cricket whose heart has seized from just a lick of the stuff. In time the rats will drown themselves with their confusion, but in the meantime I watch to make sure they don't ravage more of our store.

In Al Bayda we pick up an extra cask of gentian so that we might make bitters on the ship: to aid in digestion, to pour down the throats of the seasick, to doctor our drinks.

In a Somalian market I pick up a banana with my left hand. In India, I say the word "no." In Yemen, I grasp the sleeve-covered wrist that a woman offers to me in greeting. Once word has spread of our presence, every passable window's shade is drawn, every child is yanked inside. There is no telling what will be traded next. It seems impossible to behave ourselves. It is certain we'll offend some subtle complexity of etiquette.

In Piraeus we ask for fennel by its Greek name. "Marathon? Marathon?" We say the word to each market vendor until someone nods. It was a stalk of fennel that Prometheus used to steal fire from the gods, and when the vendor botches the exchange rate, giving us ten dozen potted fennel plants for the price of five, we feel as triumphant. Sailing out of port that night we are glad not to be chained to a rock, having our liver devoured day after day. We do not, however, escape unpunished. Within a fortnight a flutter of mouse moth larvae have hatched from the soil of the plants, and tug bites out of our woolens. They hover densely around our candles, casting the ship into unsolvable darkness.

The barrels and sacks of seed and silk, the burlap wrapping the roots of the seedlings form a pulpy poetry all their own, and on days at sea, the light shining into the hold from punched-out knots in the wood allows me to read the names stenciled on each vessel. My wife's voice rings through my head, sounding the fractured lineage of our cargo: frankincense from the land of Punt, Pippali from Kerala, sweet wood from Indonesia, amomum from Bengal. My eyes land on a bale of myrrh and I think of Berbera, where we were shown the purposeful wounds inflicted on commiphora trees to draw out the resin. All so that once we returned home our worship would have a scent all its own. In time, my wife's voice becomes dead and still in my memory. I can hear only the sounds of foreign birds made familiar over time and the many names of one spice in the disjointed language of the markets. Cinnamon, cassia, ròu gùi, cannella: they all mean the same.

When the ship's stays start to creek with the weight of our supply, we turn around. I pace the decks trying to remember my wife's name, and thinking of how to ask for forgiveness if it won't come to me. When I attempt to look back on the life that waits for me at home, the mirror reflects only on the smell of the lurching sea and the crisp-sounding snap of an aloe leaf, split and oozing focus onto my relief. I'd grown sunburned and bristled in a way that would not be familiar to her on my return. But even with as much as I'd changed, and even having lost the details of her entirely, I assumed that nothing about my wife would be different. I was sure that when I walked through that same old door, the recognition would crescendo between us and the scent of her skin would break through the curry powder and thyme and ginger, and her gentle smile would cause me to begin forgetting in the opposite direction.

Roundabout the Bottom

Until now I have been desperate and young all my life. A whirlpool's spider webbing a ship, and I am on duty, receiving the distress signals. They light up my brain with their ciphered knocking. I can only guess at what they're saying. I cheated on my Morse code tests. The water hikes itself up around them. Their noses goggle, filling with sea. They crumple deeper. The sunken six hundred struggle inside the ocean. I stay up all night thinking of ways to retrieve a ship from roundabout the bottom of the sea. I drag out maps and periscopes. I find a compass and a barometer. I can't swim, but I change into my bathing suit. I consider hurling myself off the dock and dragging each sailor up one by one. The water beetles grow fat with salt. I know it is too late, but still it's my duty to dredge them up without letting anyone know my mistake. Bells ring inside of me, telling me to do something else and then something other than that. Alarms sound. I don't know where to go. The possibilities keep splintering. My mind turns over and over like a weak ankle. The waves violin above them; a telescope can give me that sight. My marrow curdles with ignorance. I recognize my lack of reason, and I purge my apologies into the night air. I offer only my grief as recompense.

Tangle

My sister is curled around the tower like a ribbon. Venus gladdens in the sky as I try to talk her down, but seven intact sunrises later, she's still there, the solitude snarled in her hair like wind. I try to run my fingers through her disastrous ringlets but probable accidents begin to rustle between us and I give up. Dark parlors are vacant beneath her eyes and even I am praying for an aperture to open already, for some light to reach in and unknot her. A lyrical and nagging lack in me prevents me from understanding what makes her do this: like a pane of glass sanctioning off a part of my mind.

Someone deceived her; an owl perhaps.

There are pleats hidden in our heritage hiding gaps it will take much time to unfold.

There is magic all around her that does not tell the truth.

My sense of direction trembles when I get near her, like a compass near a magnet. When I try to reason with her, she yields only the half-syllables of infancy or full-martyred stories of the women who have gone before her.

I have lost my gramarye; it wriggles now somewhere in the wrong person's hands. Without it, I haven't the slightest idea how this situation will be remedied. The illogic of the good has been flossed away; malignant nonsense remains, unclaimed. I am using "nonsense" here to mean "recognition."

I have seen this happen before and prayed the nomenclature would not come back into use, that the eternal would reverse and never ask another question.

I hire a gentleman to help, to chip her fingers from the brick while I tenderly pry the ivy strands of her hair from the mortar. Her connection to this castle, chaotic and forbidden, buzzes through us like gripping a miniscule current with spit-veiled palms. We work gently and carefully, fearful of the disease patterning out to us. These gradual and tiny distances separate her from her dependence. Pulling her from this foundation is much like dislodging young poems from the beaks of hummingbirds. The power and delicacy at once astound us.

Each point connects with a rigid and forceful pulse, but as we lever her away from this landmark, she loosens, her edges going almost liquid. This work wracks our nerves, never knowing if the girl we crow from this architecture will be able to recover, will survive the withdrawal from this behemoth to which she's been clinging.

When the surrendered self of my sister lands in my arms, the true work begins. I can tell you: a fine talc settles between us and within us, evenly filling us to the brim. Our perspectives pare again and again as we fight to understand the other. We tug at the skin of each other's sentences. I find she has the looping reason of the psalmist and I know if the way I think is a library, then it is full of larks. To calm her, I weave lavender into her hair, blazed into a shock of gray at her release. When we are at a loss, we teach our mentalities ventriloquism, and find comfort in the sympathy and compassion we're able to rumble out at a moment's notice. Each day threatens whims until the petals of the town bells sound and we allow ourselves to sleep and forget.

Points on Staying Alive During That Old War

1. In the window teddy bears & alarm clocks sold themselves.
2. The gridlock stars of the night went invisible with uncertainty.
3. He asked me, Where are you going, kid, so slowly?
4. I had a way of looking back at him that made everything else clear & empty.
5. I grew tired of tongue-kissing disintegrating soldiers.
6. Like a ship's captain he wore so many buttons & so much beard.
7. His expressions showed up in the lenses of his glasses.
8. With me on the handlebars, he bandied the bicycle about dangerously.
9. Cars wrestled us on the pavers.
10. A lion and a lamb ogled our course from the lintel of the church entry.
11. Gargoyles read the palindromes of streetlights.
12. A plane raped through the low clouds of the sunset.
13. At the bar a gun stretched the distance between us.
14. We drank martinis, watched the clouds deform, and swallowed swords.
15. In general, his mouth spoke my vision & his eyeglasses circled one specific area of my brain.

16. What he ended up looking at were the places where the lace peeked through to my skin.

17. Beyond that, in a parlor, ladies wove through the crowds of wealthy men like roots looking for water.

18. Women with jazzed-out tits handed us drinks.

19. The patchwork burlap shadows listened to everything we said.

20. We walked out the door, wobbly with drink & his whistle splattered out.

21. Everything spiraled & curved like an arpeggio on the staff.

22. We played anarchist hopscotch, in the night, removing cobblestones from the sidewalks.

23. With the structure beside it felled, I could see the concrete description of the inner stairway of his apartment building perfectly.

24. I was so lost that when he put a wineglass in my hand, I held it like a map.

25. Later, drunk in his bedroom, it was as if we had hooks for hands.

26. We languished in his garret under the precarious moon.

27. We snuck down to the dark kitchen, skinned tangerines & shocked each other.

28. We were shoved full, slopped over.

29. Sweat spots metastasized on my blouse.

30. Our hands overlapped, while above us careful ghosts measured the value of appearing.

31. My bare ass on a heavily patterned carpet, designed to hide stains, and then his hand nearby.

32. We had been warned not to move from this quadrant if we knew what was good for us.

33. I was one of many who had laid herself out beside him.

34. The nights were jagged & multiple, like falling down a distracted rabbit hole.

35. My eyes exploded like stars, my lips blew wild screams his way.
36. The last of the fireworks faded. When closed, our lids replayed the whole night in negative.
37. Then nothing.
38. In the morning, with flashlights, megaphones & broad daylight we began our search again.
39. Mothers sat at home, knitting it together, the radio blaring.
40. A crowd of men judged what to do, one after the other.
41. Soldiers inflected their gunshots with meaning.
42. Two trails of smoke snuck from the same mouth.
43. A chinstrap, a seat belt, a stray hair.
44. Murky fingertips like elephant cysts.
45. Tally sheets.
46. A skull kissing a stone lion.
47. The spider web of numbers breaking down.
48. He was told to bury them where he could.
49. So many jaws pulled open by hook & key punch.
50. The general dozed while his buttons stayed alert.
51. The tentacles of his power strained wily & long.
52. Surely the planets that orbited his brain would align soon with an answer.
53. The tyranny peered over the frames of his low-slung spectacles.
54. At the dump, the pure volume of discarded motors, mechanics, coils, made my mind twist like a paper bag.
55. It never took long for the trash to gray, for the fluorescence to grow liquid brown.
56. I recorded bits of the long drawn speeches to spout back to him later.
57. He had the job of telling mothers to sit down, please turn off the radio.
58. The arthritis curled their fingers like fans of scorpion tails.
59. Each television broadcast colorful disasters.

60. Then even a kaleidoscope was too logical for what I saw & I could think of only the words "scattershot."
61. The stories he had to tell each evening to purge himself in that scrum of an attic apartment.
62. The difference between inside & out had always been tenuous for me.
63. The glare off his glasses had been mirror-slapping me for months.
64. And then that nothing.
65. His dark shadow against the window at night when I thought he was beside me.
66. A couple hours later, the bars on the windows striped his face against the pillow & I wondered how I was back here again.
67. Lately I'd been seeing even the narrowest things in panorama.
68. That was what it was like to stay alive then.
69. Those were the things I saw.
70. That was the way I moved.

Felted

The story begins realistically, with bread and wood and yarns spun.

Though hungry, the elders feed the children one fig, one filbert apiece.

After the children are reined in and sleeping under wool, the parents speak of what to do once hunger has bruised even their care for each other.

They'd been frugal, Mother argued with Father. They pulled spider webs down and packed them along the cracks in the wall for insulation. What more of a gesture could be made?

And despite all, end still stretched for end.

The children woke in the night and heard their parents come to a decision.

They knew fear when they met each other's glares; but home was not yet a place that could be left.

They knew they only needed to sleep through the night to wake up again.

So into an unlulled sleep they went, willfully hopeful.

They woke to their parents' lifting arms. Their expressions appeared stern, but behind their mother's eyes they saw that gossamer love they wanted so badly to prevail. In their father's brow they saw the prayer that this was the right decision.

And into the forest the children were driven by their parents' resignation, by the wet spring wind, by the snagging branches of the black hickory and alpine ash.

Their wool trousers blistered and their skin grew loose. The loaves of bread they carried against their hips left a trail of crumbs behind them, though they knew they would never return.

The steeples and spires and minarets of their fantasies fell through to the gutters and sewers of marshlands, the trenches of nature.

And wading through all of this circumstance, the children made this rhyme about the past:

> *Roll it over gently.*
> *Twist it on the spot.*
> *Pull it out and pull it through.*
> *Tie it in a knot.*

Entered

We is stiff and rare with the making of sense. Impressions debate the monotony. We doesn't know a needle from a conjunction. We helps the bulbs of language sprout. We learns the length of a month and the next month, it already feel short. We has sexy eyes that dawn open and the lessons murmur in keys and closets, and we reads your pale vocabulary like a limit. We eat tiny planes with our ears and telephone the world with our loud voices to notify nature of our safety. We leaves and returns, having purchased some terrible mistakes from our intricately creased elders. We lurks slightly ominous in our white van with our oatmeal and greetings and cooperation. We opens ourselves back up to the littler lives possible. The dark is waiting, relaxing, leaning into us, arriving.

    We is speaking and instancing. We opens the windows and lets the cold dedicate itself to us. The helium delays and we find a god with two bodies that swims and fishes itself through us. Geniuses is waving at us and we presses and kicks and burns and deadpans back at them. We soaks in our shame, even alone in the woodland at night. We culls our fears in promises. We leaves the evening undealt with when we can. Every day we rushes home to see what is causing the sunlight to smoke and jimmy. We is distracted by attractions.

We rests and thins ourselves out. Can we asks you something? Your thin bodies pathing circles inside us, does they ever feels like practical jokes? Can you feels the bright muscles concentrate and scatter? Can you hears the crows caw the morning open? We writes poetry the way pleasure tells lies.

A Willingness & Warning

Millie is happy here in the forest, saying "Beware," again and again. She has wept smoothly down long trails and squeezed herself into skirts of certainty and now I wouldn't be surprised if she never wants to leave. She comes up behind hikers and campers and the wayward youth whispering: "The ground shall tell all," and "The eternal lies beside you and me."

Millie grew up happy, but a switch was flipped somewhere once and then flipped back again later. What I'm trying to say is that she has known the reverse—bare and farther away from the present, still. She learned, "Murder finds time in a minute one doesn't even know is there," and also, "A minute is not long enough to ask all the questions the yellow rooms later will."

Young opinions and decisions happened everywhere and the peaceful spinning wheel of memory was catching it all. Millie would note that the man disappeared and then the next minute he would still be gone. Poems and apartments were left behind. The subway platform filled with sparrows. Everywhere. Millie thought, "I was almost a fool," and "I am swollen with caution now."

That night, Millie only got as far as the buried trains would carry her. She had heard of a land where trees grew tallest on the skyline, where the twisting days sounded only slightly, like bird calls and rustling leaves. She would find that place soon, but for now she had another strangled night to lay down with the city. The hot concrete beneath her fought the voices that passed unawares. She dreamed of nature beyond the eye of the city and of the dead plants from the hallway of her grandmother's house.

When the dew woke her, heavy on her skin, Millie found her way to her feet and her feet found her walking the questionable distance between city and country. This area looked something like a road with a small gravel shoulder. Millie was unable to see much more because she was remembering from where she'd come and imagining what was ahead. Before she knew it, a truck carrying a man traveling the world around with a load at his back had pulled up and opened his passenger door. "You're not a foolish missionary are you?" and "Don't you know there's a certain finger that works better than that one for hitchhiking?"

When they had traveled only a very short distance, Millie asked to be let out. The driver refrained from asking questions. Millie climbed out of the cab and down into the field beside them. The driver didn't wait to see if she got where she was going; he had work to do, including steering himself away from this point. Millie aimed herself at the woods beyond the field and her focus made the distance seem short. She hummed and whistled while she made her way to the trees.

Millie made herself a life of clean work and reality in the forest. She had made her mistake and now she was committed to surviving it. I have seen her. The "Beware" from her lips has landed beside me by the campfire. I can see the clean nests in the branches above me and it's easy to tell that she sleeps in a different one each night so they won't find her. When I feel her near, I say, "They've stopped looking," and "Come out now; it's safe."

More Mysteries

I let it get to the point where only shallow water filled our bellies. By that time, there was only one person to ask: my brother had just been released from rehab. I was watching to see if he'd still go awry. The throaty noise he made while we drove him home didn't bode well. He asked if he could stay with us for a day or two before going back to his own apartment. He wasn't ready to be alone.

He watched cartoons slowly, laughing a little late at the gags. I had a son, four years old, and if I didn't have the money to pay the water bill, well, daycare seemed like a joke with another adult who could spend the days with him. Jimmy had slowed since getting clean, but my desperation allowed me to believe he could manage keeping an eye on Sammy.

I worked as a custodian at the hospital. I'd scavenge the left behind, finding stuffed animals abandoned in quick transitions to the ICU, flowers to place on my table to convince myself I lived a different life, half-empty boxes of candies in rooms occupied by non-contagious patients placed on feeding tubes.

The substance of our home shook looser every day. Each morning showed a shelf sagging, its contents sliding to the ground before I noticed. I felt denied of choices, but when more than one option showed up, I broke down, so unaccustomed to being able to make the right decision.

I'd parade through the hospital like I knew the answers. I forgot whatever I could in the daytimes. I played sick pranks on myself. I attracted men with issues and put effort into keeping them around. Someone else's scars are always more mysterious. I'd invite men to sleep in my bed while my brother slept on the couch. When I went to work, everyone would still be sleeping, and according to Jimmy, my men would sleep all day. Jimmy watched cartoons with Sammy, microwaved cheese sandwiches, pretended to forget they hadn't brushed their teeth. It was a workable arrangement in the worst way.

Most of my day, I did a good job of being courteous, falling easily into the patterns of politeness. If truth had been an element, though, you'd have noticed the holes. At work, I had to write everything down: if I checked a bathroom, if I failed to mop a floor. Always a record. My supervisors would glance at it, but no one would tell me to do anything different. My thumbs peeled from the strong chemicals and I waited for someone to tell me I didn't have to come back. I'd become ambidextrous in my scrubbing. My arms were the same size. At the end of the day, I'd look hard at the ceiling while I lifted my uniform off in the locker room. I'd take a deep breath and hold it while I tied my shoes back on. I'd hold my hands under the hot water until I couldn't stand it. I'd make malfunctions I could fix.

When I got home, I'd go through the trash, looking for evidence. I wanted to know how smart Jimmy was: smart enough to stay sober or smart enough to put his empties in the neighbor's trash? I opened the bureau drawer in the kitchen, and asked him where the extra set of keys had gone. He pretended he didn't know or he really didn't. One time I came home to find him sprawled out in my nightgown—the long flowy one with the careful embroidery. He didn't fluster when I walked in the door. I widened my eyes, running them up and down his body. "This?" he said. "I wanted to get all my laundry into one load." If I hadn't just worked a twelve-hour shift, I'd have argued that I had sweatpants he could have worn just as easy. Jimmy said, "Sammy, tell your mother our new nickname for me." Sammy looked away from the cartoon cats and mice, and smiled huge. "Uncle Jimmy is Second Mommy!" I shook my head and turned back to the recliner. "That's healthy, Jim. The boy doesn't need an uncle. He needs a *second mommy?*" Jimmy cracked up and leaned over to high-five Sammy.

A few days later I found a baggie in the trash, a different size than what we bought. "What was in this?" I asked my brother. "Jeez, Kim, Sammy had a snack," he said, turning to the sink. "Where did such a snack come from, Jimmy? Not this house." "Bake sale at the park. Am I gonna get in trouble for sharing a brownie with the kid?"

If I took Sammy somewhere, Jimmy wanted to come with. I shared with Jimmy every bit of my relationship with my child now. Every opportunity I saw to nourish some small internal light I saw in Sammy was undercut by Jimmy's nudges and jokes. I wanted to pose impossible questions to Sammy to see how his youth would reason. I wanted to present him with antinomies, to see whether he would gravitate toward this thesis or that antithesis. I knew Sammy had some answers in him. Jimmy'd roll his eyes at me and tickle Sammy and tell me to lighten up—he was just a kid. At that point, I expected Jimmy to be with us a long time. Sammy was starting school at the end of summer, but I imagined the three of us carrying on. I couldn't tell if I hated it or if I was just looking for something to end, like I'd gotten used to the finite and had trouble believing in anything more.

I brought men home. I'd tell you about a single one of them if I could remember. Every night shaped itself into a fanatical bustle. Looks in the grocery store, a kind word in the hospital parking lot. I didn't spend minutes in a bar or dollars on drinks. The men always turned up over shoulders, in the bellies of shadows, at PTA meetings. Clint told me to call him. Randy told me I knew his number. Darren told me about problems he thought trumped mine, and I let them. Every time it happened I thought I was getting closer to a target and then it'd turn out I was throwing my dart in the wrong direction.

Jimmy didn't mouth off about it. He knew better. His own past sounded constant, gnarly jingles and we'd try to keep the peace as best we could. Sometimes when they were giving me a bad vibe, I told them to leave before the morning. Sometimes when their phones buzzed, I told them to go find their wives. They'd scowl at me and think better of it while I held their fate in my hands. Jimmy'd say, "No breakfast buddy today?" I'd shoot him my most dastardly glare and say, "We're allowed to do things we think better of after the fact. Am I right, brother?"

Some nights Jimmy would pace in a flurry of spells and fits—then set himself down and bite his lips, jitter his feet. Jimmy's face furrowed and dug deep at the slightest emotion. My knees sagged, soft and liquid, just like the old ladies at the public pool. Our hard lives showed up all over our bodies, but when I said something to that effect, Jimmy'd say, "Who are we comparing to?" I'd find him some aspirin, give myself a few too. We'd sip warm soda out of thin straws I stole from the coffee station at work. We'd handle each other softly for a little while. After I'd put myself to bed, I'd wake late in the night to Jim's dark whistling over the muted TV hum. The light comforted him even when the voices did not.

Twilight hung behind the curtained windows. I carried a sack of groceries that would sit on the coffee table long enough for the ice cream to melt. "Where's your uncle?" I asked him. "Jimmy?" I called into every corner of that tiny house. "He can't have gone," Sammy said. "He was just here." My stomach turned with disgust and frustration and relief. "What do you mean just here?" I asked my son. "Minutes or hours?" Sammy shrugged and turned back to the TV. The laundry basket with the broken handle where he sniffed out the clean from the dirty each morning lay abandoned beside the couch. He didn't have anything else. The bread bag sat open on the kitchen counter, half as empty as when I'd used it to make myself toast that morning. A dirty knife lay next to it, looking like it meant to make it to the sink. I'd expected worse of this moment. I looked in the trash can. "You didn't see him leave, huh?" I sat next to Sammy and stroked his baby bird hair, waiting for him to answer. At the commercial, Sammy turned to me. "How could I have seen him if he didn't go?"

Twins, or Ambivalence

The giant twins, Bittern and Barn Swallow, cannot handle the uncertain gazes that fall upon them when seen apart from each other. Their secrets exist in the negative space between them. Bittern and Barn Swallow have ears like hands reaching, mouths that curl indication into their emotions. Bittern and Barn Swallow have shirts stained with distorting drool and don't feel one bit bad about it. That's just the way their lips spill. Deep in thought, they sink slowly through mindlessness. They haul sacks of wristwatches to the Laundromat, shake the bags loose into the washers, and listen to the rattling machines drink up the mechanics of those portable clocks. Bittern and Barn Swallow don't care. They keep reaching inside for some feeling and pulling out more of their blank white stuffing. They try to believe something is possible. They keep shaking their heads and nodding, hoping one of the gestures will feel right. Every minute they feel like nervous soldiers with nothing to do. They collect useless items from garage sales, slap their dollars down, and carry away whatever is handed to them. A plastic flower, a peg doll, the sneaky thorned stem of a useless length of barbed wire. When they get home Bittern hula hoops till he's tired out and Barn Swallow fans him absently with a silk palm frond. Their eyes droop uneven and careless. Bittern and Barn Swallow look at their junk and feel nothing. They watch a space exploration special on an old black-and-white TV. Seconds into the program the spacemen arrive in space and exchange knowing smiles. Bittern and Barn Swallow look at each other, not understanding the meaning of a shared experience. In a bright and oversized world, Bittern and Barn Swallow look out of their brains, like one thing keeps fading into the next. They do not look up information in books or read magazines or have a clue what is going on anywhere. They prop themselves up on their front stoop like gargoyles and look down instead of out. So much time on those godforsaken concrete stairs, all sorts of people and things moving by, and Bittern and Barn Swallow stare at the cracks in the sidewalk. Bittern and Barn Swallow are grown but still afraid of haircuts. They pay a brave girl to come to the house and urge them to sit still and stop shrieking: it will grow back; it always does. Bittern and Barn Swallow will walk this girl home with some hope in their minds they cannot quite get around. Bittern and Barn Swallow will pick blossoms that do not belong to them. They will give the girl fingers she does not want. They will hide cherry stems, threaded needles and their tongues low inside their mouths. Bittern and Barn Swallow will share their friendliness like it's something else. The girl will get herself home. Bittern and Barn Swallow will smoke and put distance between themselves to test their limits and then hurtle back together, like losing the grip on a strip of elastic. Bittern and Barn Swallow will chew off moles that look suspicious and spit them into the gutter. They will fail to understand why it is still just the two of them leaking beside each other. They will peer into the hairdresser's window and she will try not to notice them. She will arrive at other people's homes, one hand tight around mace and the other fist clutching a horror story. Those men will live simply and long-haired a while longer and then they will attest to each other a mixture of joy and sorrow that seems to convince them they have lived long enough. They will clarify after the fact. They will decide and then forget their decision. They will remember too late that the ground has gone and fall from the sky.

Prison Windows

Roadrunner doesn't know what it is to be contained, to look at things you'll never touch, to be stacked and lined up and smeared but separate from everything else. Roadrunner and I go and see her papa in the prison, and his eyes get all yogurty and wet when he sees us. We hug hello, the fat cotton of her papa's jumpsuit scraggling against Roadrunner's skinny cotton T-shirt. I dig into my purse for the baggie of quarters and hand them to Roadrunner to buy her daddy treats. All around us, old men and penny pinchers and wise guys sit alone on one side of tables, and their families sit on the other. The laminated tile and drop ceiling remind me of cafeterias and church basements At the periphery of their vision, you can see nowhere sliding into view. All these men have the electric buzz of the catatonic stunned awake. They tell stories; they want to let their nightmares jester around in someone else's ears for a change. The edges of these men have been filed off, the guards watch to make sure of that, to ensure no sharpness comes through eager for sudden harm. I leave my cheap legs naked when we go see Roadrunner's daddy so he can have something to think about after we leave. If Roadrunner acts up, I tell her I'll sell her to the five women who live down the block, with their hats and their teeth and a neighborhood's worth of tall tales raising them up. "Roadrunner," I say, "sing your daddy the anthem; sing him that sea shanty you learned in music class," and she does, and everyone's silence sticks tight to the walls until she's finished. I stare at Roadrunner's daddy and remember well the muddy swerves of his temper when he drank too much. I remember his tongue, carnivorous and dozing against my own. I remember wishing I'd washed the floor as he laid me down and the smell of him after his suit had cooked him for an entire hot day in the sun. I have dreams and don't even try to decipher them, because as much as I want them to come true, there's as much I want to ignore and forget. I bring Roadrunner's short shoulders under my warping hands. My voice cracks and drains. The ragged engine of my tears starts up when the bell rings and it's time to go. A blue fever of sadness slugs through me as we file out onto the street. Roadrunner flips a pack of playing cards in the air and catches them. I have been tipped over. Roadrunner, with her breathy exhales, runs to the corner quick and then rushes on back to me.

The Tackiness of Souls

Minnie Fishman, burdened with a funny name by hippie parents, wants to hide in a corner at the office party, but her awareness of the wallflower cliché forces her to be social. Minnie Fishman, thirty-one, whispers in her coworker's ear that she's exhausted. She doesn't say that it's all these people who are exhausting her, that she's tired of being "on" all the time, that she's scared that if she finds someone she might actually like she'll be too jaded to connect. She finds herself at the bar with Bobby, the handsome gentlemen all of the women coo over at the water cooler. He's friendly, and it's not difficult to strike up a conversation. Bobby isn't interested because Minnie isn't a conventional bombshell and she doesn't have the confidence that must support strange beauty. Minnie isn't interested because she's talked to Bobby before and finds nothing beyond his jawbone appealing. There is no sexual tension. The jokes are lame on both sides.

Minnie excuses herself and sees the door to the pub open. It's Daniel. At the office, *Daniel* is the one *she* watches over the cubicle dividers. While sitting at her desk she can recognize the cadence of his footsteps down the carpeted "hallways" and adjusts her body language accordingly to open herself up to possible interaction. She is a producer at the ad firm. He is a creative. She thought he might not come to this holiday party, but here he is. His loose curls fall onto his thin face. He runs his hand through one side of his hair and behind the exposed lens of one of his round wire rims, his bloodshot eye rests on a purple crescent of fatigue. Daniel wears an oversized Christmas sweater with a Rudolph appliquéd on the front, complete with a light-up red nose. Before he closes the door behind him, he takes a last pull on his brown paper bag and chucks the package in a trashcan by the door. Minnie grimaces; she knows this is the sort of behavior that's endangering his position at Maximum Creata. This is someone she imagines being able to swallow whole and fears will devour her entirely if given the chance. He is the one who makes her want to empty the liquor from her belly in one go, and here he is after all.

Think the impossibility of beginning the build on a house, compare it to the decision to include Led Zeppelin in your music collection, remember trying to write your best friend's eulogy.

Minnie abandons any thoughts of leaving early. She prays being near Daniel in a social situation will create enough of a connection to get her through the night. Minnie is sure Daniel notices her and loves her back the way he loves every girl. In fact, Minnie is sure everyone likes her, or if they don't know her, they notice and *want* to like her. She hates this inexplicable vanity and recognizes its false nature, what with its being rooted in blind faith and all. She knows this, but she also never performs the resource checks on her vile delusions. Half the time she doesn't believe them herself. If the mind is a scientific article, hers will be ignored for missing references.

Think supermodels going to self-esteem therapy, compare it to Bill Gates bouncing a check, remember the advice columns in Cosmo *that suggest you play up your likable qualities to attract a man.*

Minnie's sorrowful state syncs up perfectly with Daniel's usual condition of misery. A self-diagnosed manic-depressive, Minnie's moods shift for years at a time. She makes these judgments and tells no one. Minnie has put in her time as an optimist, reading SARK, buying "Carpe Diem"–type magnets to distribute to her friends. Now, Minnie feels like a completely different person. In private she reads heavy philosophy and in public she reads whatever's been nominated for the most recent book award. Music is easier; everyone listens to sad music.

Think the subliminal enculturation of depression chic, compare it to the uniformity of "Dare to Be Different" T-shirts, remember young girls' homogenous drawings of horses.

Minnie stands by herself at the center of several groups of people, but not *in* any of them. She stands and slowly rotates on the periphery of these clusters, pretending to be enthralled by the energy surrounding her but looking a little lost. When people try to draw her into conversations, she comments on how great it is to see everyone so happy. She knows she's awkward and is convinced she likes this quality in herself because it makes everything exciting. She's happy to never know what will come out of her mouth. In this position, turning between groups, she can pretend she doesn't see Daniel approaching, but in all honesty her reason for moving around like this is so that she can keep an eye on him. She sees the red light of Daniel's sweater peripherally as it comes toward the center of the room, and soon he is standing shoulder to shoulder with her and saying nothing. If she were an honest person, Minnie would sink into Daniel with relief, but instead she holds still, nodding and smiling at a story her coworker tells.

Think an electron falling into its natural valence shell, post–"excited state," compare it to a marker and its cap snapping together, remember how fabric starts to fray only where cuts are made.

After a few moments of this direct shoulder-to-shoulder connection, Minnie Fishman makes the effort to speak. "So, I read this book, *The Lightness of Being Unbearable*, something like that—" she feels his shoulder shudder with laughter next to hers, and she continues in her nervously proper voice, "—and I was looking for someone to talk to about it."

Think of the constant running script of conversations that might occur, compare it to the coupling of scissor blades and the benefit of this marriage, remember Henry Miller and Anais Nin.

Minnie and Daniel have spoken before. In all honesty, they kissed at last year's Christmas party, but Minnie can't be sure Daniel even remembers that. They were both *soused*. Just months before Daniel came to work in a T-shirt she recognized as being from her elementary school, and the coincidence was too great for her to keep her mouth shut. She asked where he'd gotten it, expecting to hear he'd happened upon it in a thrift store. Instead she learned that he'd just stopped seeing a girl Minnie had gone to school with. She did the math and discovered Daniel and his girlfriend must have still been together when he and Minnie had shared that kiss last December. Since then they'd nodded to each other when passing and occasionally eaten lunch together.

Think meeting someone and realizing they've lived in the build-ing next door to you for years, compare it to the drone of the emer-gency broadcast system, remember the fear of being buried by the possibility of words and being scared into silence.

Minnie had been sitting in the lunch room a few weeks ago. Daniel sat down with a Hot Pocket and asked her, "Do you read?" Minnie knew he knew she read and was a snob about words and their usage. Minnie had been crowned "The Queen of the Red Pens" for the way she hacked at the advertising copy. Minnie knew he expected her to say, "Of course," so instead she said, "Never." She couldn't hold it though and her disgusted scowl collapsed into a broad grin. He told her he'd just read *The Unbearable Lightness of Being* and he was thinking of starting a company book group. She nodded, seemingly indifferent, but as soon as she got home that night, she ordered the book. When it arrived she read it in one night. It may have been that she knew as soon as she read it she would have a reason to talk to him again. However, the thought of speaking to him, let alone coming up with intelligent things to say about a book, terrified her. Several months earlier she'd decided she needed to read all of the books on her shelf she'd been meaning to get around to. Each night she made her dinner and settled into the couch until she'd finished or fallen asleep, but sleep had been elusive lately. The books were an excuse to ignore the problem.

Think deliberation disguised as psychosis, compare it to scoffing at laughter from the apartment next door, remember the claustrophobia of a syllogism.

Back in the smoky, moist barroom, Minnie receives the response to her inquiry: a shoulder shrug and a smirk from Daniel.

Think of it as a metaphor for the future of this relationship, compare people who are smart to the ones who are hungry, remember that time your ex-boyfriend called you masochistic and how it made you feel accomplished.

Minnie shakes her head and walks away from his cryptic and lackluster response. An hour later she sits in a booth with co-workers and they are screaming along to some song that she loved when she was a teenager. They're dancing in their seats—violently enough that they will feel an unfamiliar twist in their backs tomorrow. Daniel sits down next to her and grabs her hand and plants his face inches from hers. Minnie stops singing, but Daniel goes on. He sings and sings and Minnie manages to maintain both eye contact and her cool until the guitar part comes up and he leans in to whisper, "I bet I can freak you out."

Think of being one "yes" short of severely depressed on the online mental health scale, compare it to how you have to collapse as much air as you can from your lungs before you can use an asthma inhaler, remember you haven't eaten anything but candy canes for the last ninety-six hours.

Minnie doesn't blink as she says, "Too late." She is drunk and the heels of her shoes are skinny. She stumbles over him, out of the booth. She's out the door and on the street before

Daniel has even straightened his legs. He catches up as she climbs into a cab and he crawls in after her. This isn't what Minnie Fishman wants, but she also doesn't tell him to get out. When they get to her apartment, he tries to follow her and she says, without looking at him, "Let me know when you get home safely."

Think about all that business touting medium as message, compare it to statues whittled away to their craggy essence at the art museum, remember shouting, "Just kiss her already" at the movie screen.

Back in her apartment, Minnie crawls into a leotard and huge black pants. She's too keyed up to sleep. She puts some music on and dances, low to the ground and primitive. The phone breaks the flow.

Think how words become benign in languages you don't know, compare it to the satisfaction of a twist ending, remember smashing your forearm against the doorknob accidentally and admiring the deep shades of the bruise.

"Minnie?" Daniel says. She asks if he got home okay, and of course he did. Daniel tells Minnie how happy he is they left. He tells her he can't stand being around people lately but that he felt like he had to go to the work party, to put in an appearance and see if his feelings had changed. Minnie silently hates him for being the same as her, wishes neither of them were this self-centered. Her body bends to the memorized height of her couch cushions. They talk for an hour, and then Daniel asks Minnie what she's doing. Minnie doesn't answer. He knows. "Do you want to go to the Golden Nugget? I'm starving." She says, "Just let me get my jacket," and hangs up without waiting for details. Finally, she feels powerful.

Think the fulfillment of peeling dried glue off your hands, compare it to a reverse-reverse psychology, remember that your definition of criticizing ads has always been to underline the phrases you like and the words you don't.

Minnie waits outside her building twenty minutes later, face scrubbed clean and her tousled hair scraped into a neat ponytail. Clear and flat. He pulls up in his blue car, hubcaps gone. Minnie climbs into the car, the stereo playing cheesy pop, not what she expected. They drive and listen to the music, and in a minute the CD stops. "Happens in the cold," Daniel says. They ride the rest of the way getting by on grunts and quick exhalations. Both are overcome with nerve and reservation because they know the truth of the noises the other is emitting. They pull into the lot and no one moves.

Think of the tense of your calves before you jump in the shark tank, compare it to red eyes showing up in photographs, remember the definite end to the warmth from the heaters of this '93 Grand Am when its engine is off.

Minnie is relieved that Daniel waits while she navigates the faulty passenger seat belt, but happier he doesn't hold the Golden Nugget door open for her. Minnie hates chivalry because she doesn't possess the presumption to demand it at all times. They sit down. It is empty and four a.m. The waitress takes their order. Daniel orders a skillet and a cup of coffee. Minnie orders chocolate milk, and Daniel's face eases into a smile before he collapses with a whimper into his hands.

Think the orphanage of newspapers on the subway, compare it to Dutch elm disease, remember how easy it is to become a skilled liar.

"Minnie," he moans, "tell me to take you home right now. I'm a mess." Minnie squints at him and asks what's wrong. Daniel's forehead lands on the edge of the table with an "I don't know." Minnie smiles attentively, but she's thinking, "Is this what I'm like?" Their food arrives. Daniel pulls himself together for the waitress, lifting his head and blinking at the light. Minnie stirs the chocolate into her milk and takes a big gulp. She licks the syrup off her spoon. Daniel pours lots of cream and sugar into his coffee and smiles at Minnie. She places the spoon in her mouth and sucks it even after no chocolate remains. Though it appears as if she is relishing it, her eyes nearly tip their reserve of tears.

Think the way going to see a shrink would be irreversible, compare it to the incapacitation of a fireplace with no chimney, remember the easy happiness you gained from dinosaurs as a child.

Daniel hands Minnie a black-and-white composition book. He tells her she is the first to see it. Minnie feels honored and skeptical in equal parts as she begins flipping through. The first thing she finds is an unfinished letter to his ex-girlfriend, telling her he misses the way her heels dug into his calves. Something twists inside her. She's sure this isn't where she's supposed to be at all, but she stays. Minnie pages through the notebook, thinking she should have gotten this out of her system in high school or college. Daniel can tell she's distracted and makes Minnie read a story aloud because he thinks she's not actually reading.

Think the way you skip tedious sonnets to get to "For I am shamed by that which I bring forth / And so should you to love things nothing worth," compare it to being wrong about something you fought so hard for, remember how a friend of yours told you he used to run through Central Park in the middle of the night to test fate.

Two hours later, Minnie is arranging silverware into architecture. Daniel talks about Hegel and the waiter bussing the table across the section appends Daniel's reference, eager to show he is more than a night-shift employee. The waitress brings the check, and Daniel takes it. Minnie decides not to quibble over the price of chocolate milk. Daniel pays the bill while she runs into the bathroom. A moment later, she looks at her bright face in the fluorescent mirror. She smiles, exaggerated and toothy, and then her face unfolds itself into blankness.

Think of scars from impatience with scabs, compare it to the exhausted, disoriented genius of the last minutes of a football game, remember how you can now completely ignore the ceaseless purr of electricity everywhere.

Daniel is talking to the cashier when Minnie comes out of the bathroom and she waits for him to finish his conversation. Minnie's biceps tense to cross her arms as Daniel holds the door open for her and she explodes into a sprint to the car. Daniel takes his time finding his keys and easing into the vehicle.

Think Aesop's character foils, compare it to the tackiness of the concept of souls, remember the tension of condescension.

Minnie watches him reach across the passenger seat and unlock her door. She thanks God he doesn't pull the handle. She jerks in as the cold quickly immobilizes her joints. The engine starts and they drive in silence until suddenly the CD kicks on again and it's the same sappy pop song. Minnie laughs. Daniel says earnestly, "This is the saddest song in the world." Minnie can't help herself and disagrees. Daniel says they will drive around until she admits how depressing the song is.

Think the swipe of a credit card, compare it to the minor distortions of the shadow of bricks on the mortar separating them, remember how this song was sappy the first time you heard it and some things never change.

Around the fourth rotation, Minnie finally admits the song is heartbreaking because it's 6:30 in the morning and she never seizes moments this easy. Daniel takes her back to her apartment. Minnie sits in her seat silent for several minutes. He asks her what she's thinking. Minnie says, "Really?" and Daniel just looks at her. "I was counting the number of times you said the word *pertinent* tonight." She smiles tentatively. He frowns and turns away, nodding. Minnie takes her time getting out of the car. Daniel says nothing.

Think needing permission to be happier, compare it to stopping yourself before you say something stupid and then saying it anyway, remember all you've wanted in this world is for one person to call you "home."

Minnie disappears into the vestibule door for the second time tonight and calls his house before he gets home. On his answering machine she reads a story about being able to figure out what's good and what's bad.

Think telling someone he shouldn't jump off that ledge for your sake instead of his own, compare it to the invasion of an epitaph, remember bedtime stories.

Hospitable Madness

A chatelaine so full of tools delicate to a task should reveal what said person does with her measured time.

And yet, along with the tiny snips and bucket of a thimble, there hung a compass, a pocket watch, a skate key, a touch wood, and several other metallic objects of antiquity.

"The worst attraction," she said, settling carefully onto the settee, "is to the everyday."

We nodded, attempting careful equations behind our eyes, hoping our guest wouldn't notice.

"My work is not why people die."

When our gaze returned to her, she seemed closer.

"Tonight, I carry out a plan of nervy education." She pulled a felt-wrapped bundle from the carpet bag at her feet.

The host took my hand in his. Each word was a surfacing fin. We were surrounded.

"When *I* die, I will die happy, because I will die doing what I love." She began to unroll the felt. With the first tumble, a knife stretched out. With each subsequent movement of her hand the felt unfurled another blade.

She stood, grabbing handfuls of knives. "If something goes wrong, don't tell me." Her fists hung at her sides and she breathed deeply. Then, like nothing at all, the daggers were in the air. They framed her like rays of light surrounding a saint. As they fell, she caught each one and sent it back up. She danced and the chatelaine tinkled sweetly, lightening the mood of the knives' silent flight.

The host released my hand and began to clap vigorously. In each slap of one palm against the other I heard his relief, but I'm sure she listened only to the pure praise she desired so. The host elbowed me, urged me to do the same, and yet I was still quite certain this would not be the end.

Prowlers

On the radio we'd heard about a trend in nature in which wolf packs were growing larger and larger—expanding into super packs. The packs were impossible to fight off. They'd attack one small animal and share the meat among them, then find another prey. It was like the wolf version of small plates. These super-packs were forming everywhere. There was one apparently on the prowl right in the area we were driving through. The car protected us, but we'd need to stop for gas some time.

We drove from Chicago to Albuquerque. This was the time I caught a ride with a friend of a friend of a friend—someone far enough removed that you'd doubt the truth of any of their stories, were I to tell 'em. As luck would have it, though, twenty-two hours passed with neither of us finishing a thing we had to say. We kept getting interrupted by roadside attractions, something on the radio, a cop pulling us over. Tale after tale cut short, so there's no reason to retell 'em or to disbelieve 'em.

This friend of a friend, people called him "Coot." I was too embarrassed to ask him his real name, and what would it have mattered?

We were both victims of well-wrought curiosity. Coot wanted to make his way to Sedona to see about some crystals. I heard about the chance of a cheap ride, and the word Albuquerque tripped off my tongue. I gave a rent check to my roommates and packed a bag full of fluorescent jean shorts and T-shirts covered in paint-soaked handprints. It was that decade. Coot and I displayed our suspicion of each other plainly, but the price of gas would be halved, and my friends of friends vouched for both me and him. I wouldn't run off with the car or rifle through his belongings. He would get me there.

I had a boyfriend who'd just broken up with me, but that wasn't unusual. He and I loved in a way that was always between talks, punctuated, alive. This might get old for some people, but it kept us going. His name was Wade, but I called him Wader. He hated it for being a homophone, but liked that I'd awarded him a nickname. When Wader heard about me spending twenty-two hours in a car with Coot, he begged me to stay, but even his sobbing didn't drag me closer to him. The ten inches of black space between us on the couch stayed constant, until I hoisted my duffel onto my shoulder at the sound of Coot's car horn. "I'll write when I get there, Wader," I said and he looked up at me, always dramatic, and said, "Well, if those don't sound like dying words." Trying not to let that sentence dot my mind, I threw my bag in the back seat and forced a smile at Coot.

Empty plastic bottles covered the floor of the car. "What do you say I pitch all of these the next time we stop for gas?" Across the dashboard, Coot had lined up twenty-two cat figurines. I counted 'em. "I know we don't know each other so well, but there are exactly as many cats as there are hours we'll be in this car." Coot grunted and kept his eyes on the road. I would learn that he wasn't one for believing in coincidences.

In the glove compartment I found a pistol that felt heavy, but Coot scoffed at my foolishness, telling me it was a toy. My stomach dropped down into the pile of plastic bottles, but Coot said, "Go ahead. Fire it at me. That's how afraid you should be of that thing." I refused his offer, and clicked the compartment shut again.

When it was my turn to drive, I counted the seconds between signs on the highway to stay awake. In more populated areas, I waited for the negative light of the sodium streetlamps to shine in on us, catching glimpses of the filth coating every surface of the car and our skin.

I tried to talk Coot into telling stories, but he'd trail off and pass out in the passenger seat or get himself distracted behind the wheel. I'd try to tell him stories, but he wasn't much of a responder, so I'd get bored and flip the radio on, and he'd never complain that he wanted to know what happened. How did I get home that night? What was in the water? Who was at the door after all? Then on the radio, that story of the wolves came on. I couldn't tell if Coot had heard it, but I grew nervous. When I switched the station to something I could sing along to, Coot shut the radio off. I could take a hint.

My friends back home wondered why I was going to Albuquerque. It couldn't just be for the name, they said. "I need to feel some control," I'd admit. I'd become so accustomed to stinking and failing that I wanted to set a goal I couldn't fuck up. I could mess up a job opportunity easy. I could complain that I'd never get a painting just the way I wanted it. But to move my body from Chicago to Albuquerque and back felt like an easy and satisfying thing to do. "What will you do when you get there?" friends of friends asked. "Find a little proof and head on home,"

I'd reply, and more often than not, they'd say they were going to grab another beer and ask if I'd like one. When they returned with the two bottles, they'd have a story to tell about some quarrel they'd had earlier that day and we'd drift away from the need to understand why I was leaving.

I asked Coot questions, and mostly he remembered he didn't care to talk to me. But a few times he responded automatically. He'd been convicted of a felony, a fact I think he was trying to scare me with. He told me it was better I didn't know what. I said I thought it was my right to know, and he said, if anything, what he was convicted of made this car ride safer. I asked if he'd been in jail, and he said, "Um, that's how that works, yes." I was still pretty certain there was some wiggle room there, but if he wanted to play it like the two were unavoidably linked, then that was his call.

That same radio story came on about the wolves again. I shut it off and pulled out a sketchbook to doodle: several young boys tied to railroad tracks, a dirty man on a city apartment stoop, a full train showing a man with an empty seat beside him. Coot glanced at the drawing and said nothing. I tried to tell him a story about how I almost died. How I'd gotten very sick and how long it had taken me to notice how sick I was. How by the worst point I hadn't showered in weeks, and I'd stopped leaving the house. How I didn't notice that no one was calling me and I wasn't calling anyone either. I waited for Coot to ask me what had been wrong, but I quieted down, and his voice never emerged. He filled with refusal. I learned that a skull doesn't equal a mind.

I was still sleeping when Coot pulled into a roadside motel in Albuquerque. I heard the gravel of the lot locating itself beneath the car, and my voice caught. "Where is this?" I asked, and Coot said, "This is where we part." I climbed out of the car and walked toward the office. He called after me that I'd forgotten my bag. I'd thought he would at least wait for me to be sure I could get a room, but I was meek, and I pulled open that sticky back passenger door and grabbed my belongings. As the door to the office tinkled open, I heard his tires squeal back onto the road.

That afternoon I wrote Wader to let him know I was safe in Albuquerque. I signed the letter "Love, Jovey" because that's what I felt at the time. When I returned to Chicago everything would be muddier, but that sign-off felt clear and true that morning.

I've made a lot of mistakes, and mostly, I've been able to recognize them as such. That drive, though, something was wrong, and I've never been able to figure it out. There's an old Hitchcock movie where all of the violence happens behind a curtain. A man pulls a woman behind heavy velvet and tries to rape her. The camera shows her hand fumble out grasping for anything to defend herself, until her fingers land on a knife left out on a cheese board, and that, too, disappears behind the curtain. And then, the lumpy, unseen struggle subsides, and you see a male hand flop out, over the arm of a chair, and the terrified heroine emerges, wondering how what just happened could have happened. All that confusion and she was the only one to survive to tell the story. No one could make it clearer for her. She had all the answers there could be.

Filch and Rot

We started out as petty thieves, picking up the mulch-worthy crabapples from neighbors' lawns. We poured water into the vodka bottles in the basement. We took swipes of our brothers' deodorant to cover up our sour smells because it had a better scent than anything the pharmacy had to offer us young ladies.

We fished the tubes of lipstick out of our teachers' purses. They all wore the same brand: CoverGirl TruShine. In a town with so few options, why were they ignoring the other brands in the drugstore aisle? Surely some teacher with some popularity had spread the word that TruShine was the best product and all of the other teachers had trucked over to the Walgreens or the CVS to smear samples on the thumb edge of their hands.

While our parents watched movies or failed to listen to each other in arguments, we tucked out the back doors. We set up shell games on the street with the lipstick. We'd uncap the tubes and spin out the shades.

Mrs. Ball wore muted Powderpink Shine and applied hers until the waxy stick ended in a flat plateau. Mrs. Pullman wore Blushberry Shine and rounded off the tip of her tube. Finally we flashed Ms. Withers' whorey, bright crimson Valentine Shine with the perfectly maintained diagonal. *Cosmo* had told us this shape of lipstick proved that Ms. Withers was the moody, daring role model we all hoped she was, riding around town with the young shop teacher, his hands rough and smelling of oil, his eyes full of promises and splinters.

We'd cap the tubes and lay them down on our piece of cardboard outside the Circle K. Our hands would move fast, sliding the tubes around each other. "Powderpink Blushberry Valentine!" we'd call like we were conjuring something. Cash had been laid down. How our parents never heard about the con girls shuffling lipstick outside the Circle K, we didn't know, and thanked the Good Lord above out loud, but in each of our minds we thought, "Someday they'll hear and they'll need to confront us, and would that be so bad?"

We were fast with our hands. We'd rotate in Rosy Shine and Mauve Shine that looked so much like Powderpink Shine. We'd shake our heads sadly when the mark picked the wrong shade every time. "Just tell me how you do it," Bobby's father asked us, but we knew if we didn't tell him that he'd come back with a theory, empty his wallet again.

It wasn't long before we started picking up other people's orders at the fast-food chain. One of us would order a soft drink and we'd sit with our backs turned to the people line. We'd wait to watch a harried mother pass us to settle her children in before the food was up, and when that number was called and the mother was still pulling off her children's coats and digging up one more booster seat, three of us would file out. One would go smile sweetly at the young pimpled boy who went to school in the next town over and wrap her neatly manicured fingers slowly around the top of the bag, and say, in a voice so breathy it would blow through the boy's twitchy dreams, "Thank *you*," and meet us outside where we'd walk to the forest preserve and eat the bits of chicken and plain hamburgers ordered for the kids and the fish fillet sandwich the mother had fooled herself into thinking was a favor to her health.

We had been the smart girls, but we'd started getting pretty and thievish. We used our smarts to find workarounds instead. If we only had time to write two pages of a five-page research paper, we printed out the pages we had and then stapled them to three blank pages, and ripped those pages off, leaving a jagged triangle of paper where no more research had been. We'd slide this paper into the middle of the pile, and by the next day or the next week when the teacher had sorted through the papers, she would have to tell us she was so sorry, but it appeared some of the pages of our reports had been lost, could we please reprint them and turn them in ASAP, and we said we'd bring them the next day.

Shanna kept saying, "So we bought some time. What's the big deal?"

"Stole. *Stole* that time," I reminded her.

We started cutting class and trolling other neighborhoods,. watching people's routines. We noticed people loading their cars with suitcases. We counted family members leaving the house. We had a pattern down. Janna checked all the windows. Eve checked all the doors. Cathy looked for spare keys, and I sat out front ready to call out if I saw something suspicious. We never went in without an escape route, an alley or some woods behind the house that we could disappear in.

We took TVs until we had enough of those. We took jewelry and movies we wanted to see and bottles of liquor and stuffed animals that stared at us saying, "Take me with you!" We could have taken a lot more with the intention of selling it, but we behaved modestly. Most of all, it was the thrill we were stealing.

We rubbed dirt into the hems of our skirts and dusted our sandaled feet until they were an ashy gray. At home we exclaimed our wonder at what people would throw away or drop off at the dump. Our fathers smiled at the new TV, but our mothers knew that any self-respecting proprietor of the trash heap would have kept that TV for himself. "Eleanor, you can't keep a stuffed bunny from the dump. You'll get red fever or cholera." She pronounced "cholera" with a "ch," and when we heard that noise our minds felt vindicated. We'd shrug and hug the animal tight, then place it in the arms of our little sister, and she'd run off thrilled and our mother would give us a look like, "You've just murdered your sister. Hope you're happy." And we were. Not because we were killing our sisters but because we knew how our mother was failing.

In the winter, we'd plan. The snow slowed us down. We had big downy coats to hide our bounty in, but we hadn't figured out how to avoid leaving footprints around the houses. We barreled around each other's rooms, sifting through the jewels we'd purloined, letting loose an expensive kind of laughter. Our mothers would knock on our doors, convinced we were getting high. When no smells shaped the right way they'd walk around the outside of the house looking for our windows to be open, for toilet paper tubes with dryer sheets to be aimed out into the winter air, but they were always shut tight. We saw our mothers in the side yards making tracks of their own and we waved enthusiastically, the wide expanses of our faces undamaged by fear of being caught. Our mothers inhaled sharply, their nostrils stamped together by the freezing wind, their khakis wet to the knee from not having bothered to put boots on instead of house sneakers. When our friends left, our mothers would ask to talk to us. "Are you involved in hate and destruction?" they'd ask. They'd comment on the asymmetry of the family as we grew and distanced ourselves. They began worrying and we all felt moments of sympathy for them, but we shook our heads just the same. "Is this what it is to watch your daughter grow?" they asked themselves as we walked away from the table. We shaped our fingers into guns as we rounded the corner and shot at our heads.

We stole all the photos of ourselves from this time. We stole our mothers' passwords and deleted the photos of us off their computers, and slipped pictures out of the frames lining the halls.

"No," they'd say with big worry in their voices. "This is the end. I'm putting up with your secrets, but I won't let you take my memories." Our mothers would hunt our rooms for them to no avail. We didn't think about how someday we'd like to look at who we were. Our mothers hugged us tightly, trying to convince us to return to our old selves, the selves in those photos. "You're soaked through," they'd say, but it was our mothers who were coated with sweat like dishes too early out of the dishwasher, squeaky and startled. It is not uncommon for a person to first imagine someone else showing their symptoms in an attempt to objectify the pain and disease.

Our mothers told us we smelled naked and ripe, and when they got close enough to hold an ear to our hearts they recreated the burbling with wet sounds, their clammy tongues flicking around their mouths.

"Decay," we whispered outside their other ears. All those manners and ethics were being pulled loose of us like too many bones, coyotes and vultures burying them deep to savor at a later time.

First the lifeblood drains to the dependent parts of our consciences and that lividity rises up behind our expressions. The muscles of our decency refuse to uncouple. Our honor cools to a temperature of consensus.

Froth and rupture. Our minds pillage themselves. New colors marble through the veins of our principles. Our hair slides out. Our skin slips. The maggots feed on us and squirm away to make their own code.

We'd turned rotten is all. Autolysis and putrefaction. Our morals were breaking themselves down. Blistering. Aided by the outside world that hunted out any point of weakness to feed on. Bloating. All that integrity *burglarized* by blowflies and filched by gut flora. A vibrant person will rebuild herself. Only the dead break down.

Recipe for Her Absence

Ingredients:
  1 Half-Empty Bottle of Perfume
  1 Glass of Water

Directions:
   When she gets up to leave, think of everything. Try to bribe
her, blackmail her, hold objects for ransom. Objects like that al-
most-empty bottle of perfume she's had in your medicine cabinet
since it was full. When she looks at you like you're crazy, grip
your fearful fingers tighter around the bottle and shove it into
your pocket defiantly. Turn around so you don't have to watch
her leave for the last time. When the screen door slams shut and
then slams shut a little less and then wobbles, take the perfume
from your pocket and figure out how to work the cap. Does it
twist? Does it snap? Does it just lift right off? Yes. Spray the perfume into the air in front of your face and sneeze a little and be
thankful for that small regularity. Every morning, every evening,
when she left the house, she would perform this ritual, and if you
were standing nearby you would sneeze, and right now that con-
vulsion feels more comfortable than your skin. Cup your palm a
little. Hold the bottle to your nose and breathe in deeply. Feel the
tears rise and squeeze them back into yourself. Hold the bottle
close to your cupped palm and spray it until a little puddle exists.
Lean your face down to your palm and lap it up like a kitten.

Grimace. Remember what it was like to lick the Windex off the window that time when you were a child. Lick your hand until the perfume is gone. Shake your hand dry. Flex your tongue out of your mouth. Savor the bitter alcohol and flowers. Think about how everything is different now, how from now on this perfume will be this taste and not her smell. Panic and think about the long list of irreversible things you've done. Go to the kitchen and fill a lukewarm glass of water. There is no time to wait for the cold to meander to the tap. Drink the glass down and then spit onto the stacks of dirty dishes you've been meaning to do. Already, allow the lazy hindsight to come into focus: how she could plow you down with her comments, how in every picture you could detect dangerous lies, how she'd stack the decks every time you played gin and deny it again and again. The pungent perfume on your tongue reminds you that no matter how sweet you remember her smelling, when you think of the taste of her now, your tongue will remind you of the perfume lingering at the back of your throat.

Despite your best efforts, remember that ridiculous night in Grasse when you drank too much good French wine in the café, and how strong the summer breeze was on the short walk back to the hotel, and how she had that loose dress on that the wind nearly knocked off, and how her ankle turned gently on the cobblestones and how instead of leaning to help her up, you stretched yourself out on the ground beside her and twined yourself into her spilled limbs, and how you lay there breathing in the moist Provence air, clean and fragrant, and how she imagined aloud the wind undressing the flowers in the fields that surrounded the town, and how when you kissed her bare shoulder, you swore you could taste the jasmine on her skin.

Now try and remember the taste of the perfume in your palm.

Both Fruit and Flower

Ciara-Bianca, Ciara-bright, Ciara-blossom turned to fruit.

Every day Ciara-Bianca is cross-pollinated, self-surprised, she stays the same and comes undone.

Ciara-Bianca, at twilight, can feel herself turn waterless, feel her bones bend into beams of ghost and question, can feel the transformation occur, a little backwards shipwreck.

In the dark of night she is the ruins of ancient artwork. In the morning, she is a mystery, even in full light. As the afternoon turns to evening, though, she can feel herself become the ultimate skeleton fiction.

It's at twilight that the buzzing of the day embeds itself in her, changes her. It's at twilight when her stamen feels the hunger, and her pistil feels full; the sticky tip of her stigma pulling the full day deep into her. That is when her body begins to make the apple seeds.

Ciara-Bianca, on the stage, under the gas lamp of faithless vision and the panic of crushed myth. She drums closed arguments with faint questions. She cannot shake it out.

The petals of the blossom fall as she plumps, her skin growing thinner, building layer on layer, until that epithelial first coat has knotted itself into a core.

Ciara-Bianca rising round the neck of the dying spring, shining from within like startled death, her vivid veins rushing like nothing when compared to the famous, clean poetry of the fresh curse of fruit.

At the bottom of her are all the furry parts that made her, the part we try to ignore, to pretend it doesn't mar the smooth red slick of the separation of inside and out.

Ciara-Bianca, filled with people weary of the great half dark, in her hands rests a cold story.

A little overripe, looked over, winked at and passed on, the chiaroscuro of Ciara-Bianca jumps with centipedes. She can only feel love like a loose shadow.

"When I've rotted," Ciara-Bianca tells herself, "when I'm past possibility, I plan on asking what all of this is about. I'll do it, in the service of shrill facts and likely twins. I'll give credence to the sunless ideas, beautifully explained under the weight of many men and women. I'll win my case with that old repellant weapon: betrayal."

Ciara-Bianca, like church or scorpions, bent and strange, cut with a little bit of snake oil. Ciara-Bianca says, "It'll all be over in the end."

Even a roof is under something. Even the coldest day has a cooler shadow, grateful and long. Even the deepest hole can be dug deeper.

In her bed, in the pitch black, Ciara-Bianca can hear everything. The memory of her is thrown away just as it is called into being.

In the dark of the night Ciara-Bianca's face becomes the moon becomes a chemical fire becomes a belly of dead moisture becomes herself and her.

Which is true? Ciara-Bianca could flower and bear fruit at once, could watch herself without touching a mirror, could read her story without laying eyes on the page.

Configuration

"Holy God," we say. Lory has crinkled all of the wire hangers into a meaningless Venn diagram on the wall. Lory tries to wink and tit in some sort of meaningful way, but she is covered in flowers and downy hair, and it all feels like too much to be honest. Lory, standing on top of the covers, like some conquest, Lory hears out of one ear and pouts against her shallow chin. "Lory," we say. "Go ahead, explain it." But Lory knows the rules. Lory presses the meaning deep inside her and reaches with a blunt thumb between her teeth to dig something out. "Come in," she says. "Take a look." And that's all we do. We whisper, and Lory beams proudly and stirs within herself. We coo a bit and think that we'll forget this by tomorrow, but a handful of tomorrows come and this image still pops up like floaters in our vision.

The next time we see Lory, Tuck is disappearing behind her, doing that thing where you stand behind someone and stick you arms under their armpits so it looks like the person in front has four arms. We wait for them to get still before we laugh, and their elbows are waving and tangling again, and then we have to fly our hands to our faces, because the image of those wire hangers returns. Lory, with her piggish eyes, looks down, and sees all four of her arms, and tells us twice about her confusion headaches. Tuck sends out a stray hum behind her, to remind her he's there, and her arms get heavy and trap his hands right where they are. The two of them stand for hours there, free and yet tied. We leave and go to the mall, where there are salesgirls and gold and the slow pace of age. There are hollow prayers in the air that look just like window shopping. We hop around in our slender skins and ogle the sagging, elderly patrons on the benches. We stick out like sore thumbs, or the old people do. Whichever it is, someone doesn't fit in.

The Effects of Rotation

In this messy room, three rumpled girls toss themselves down on misshapen couches, melting with their ignorance of enterprise. Their eyes loll around lazily, never stopping. Their arms drape down to the bubbling shag carpet. Soft tufts of breath emerge from their pillowy cheeks as their minds move nowhere. In this loose, open ocean of a room, three slugs will never even know what it is to scrape their full bellies along concrete or punch pulpy holes into the tissue of fruit. Torsion is taking hold of their insides, twisting them to make explanations for the doctors, who haven't a clue.

The Things Which Blind Us

I hated when they made me wear the bear suit in public and hated it more for how comfortable it was when I was alone. A conundrum. The heat had been turned off in my apartment for almost a week. Wearing the bear suit in public wasn't making enough money for me to pay the bill, but it kept me pretty warm. If I quit to find another job, I would have to return the bear suit, and then how would I sleep? I avoided making a decision, which meant deciding to keep the bear suit and living without heat.

At that point, I'd been confused for days, like trying to see through dense foliage. I hoped it was just the mescaline wearing off. When that effect faded, suddenly, random birds began falling from the sky every few minutes, and when I looked for them near the ground, they were nowhere. When my coworker offered me another of the small pills at the drive-in several weeks later, I declined. It was warming up. I was thinking of ditching the bear suit. Not only did I not need it in my apartment, but it was getting miserable to be inside of the suit on the hot sidewalks all day passing out sale flyers.

I lived on the fourth floor of a big semi-converted warehouse and my best friend lived on the fourth floor of the building across the alley. I spent that summer trying to rig passageways between our windows. First, I thought big and worked on designs for a rope bridge. By the end of the summer it was just a tin can telephone, and even that proved to be tricky.

My friend and I crowed open the door of the landlord's storage space downstairs, convinced he'd been stealing from me. We navigated the dark basement, through unknown detritus, and then, as we got deeper in, our eyes adjusted. With the blindness arrived a sensation in which everything I touched felt like something I had owned. Then lights seemed to click on in my brain and everything I touched was bright and clear. And then everything took shape, or real light appeared again, and it was fantastic. A whole scene unfolded as if another world existed in that basement: there were tattooed ladies and strongmen slumping in laps around carousels and Ferris wheels, carnival barkers presenting me with fantastic options, everything wound and rotating. I looked at my friend, to share our amazement at what was hidden in this basement, but she was unfazed, unaware of the circus spinning behind her. She was still looking with her hands for anything that had once been mine. Suddenly, I felt very alone, sure I was seeing everything which blinded the rest of the world. In the darkness, from the light of the carnival, I looked at my friend, and she held up a set of magnets she'd given me, not even freed of their packaging yet, which had gone missing weeks ago. They were ugly, some bubble sticker of a teen TV-movie character pasted onto an oversized paperclip, some kind of joke I didn't get. I hadn't been upset to lose them specifically, but they were not the landlord's to take. My mind started wandering to how often he went into my apartment, wondered if he had been hiding behind the shower curtain while I danced in the bear suit to keep warm. "I think I found the birthday gift I gave you," my friend said. Her hands were running all over the package, figuring it out. She still couldn't see. We pocketed the proof and lifted our knees high over the stacks of old newspapers, dirty piles of rags, stained fish tanks. I looked back for the fair before we left, but it was just that blank slate of darkness we'd seen when we'd first cracked the door.

Later that night we terrorized the open galleries down the street. Art had metastasized on walls which had been blank days before. Photographs of people wearing scrappy helmets that looked like weapons. Sculptures that triggered my gag reflex, a disgusting network of roots and plugs extending from the undersides of everything. Paintings of rockets announcing themselves against absurd skies, everything reminding me of a time when the world seemed covered in gluey strings of resistance and life had me convinced I needed a reason to do anything I got it in my brain to do.

On the way home, my friend looked up into the sky and told me about how the planets would dissolve from one side to the other until we could stare straight into their hollow centers. I shoved her and we didn't bother saying goodnight before we climbed to our respective towers.

Back in the apartment, alone, unable to sleep, I spent the night making myself sick, spinning in a loose office chair. I spent time running my hands over my body looking for that lovable cancer monster. I convinced myself I was full of putrid and secretive cells. I thought about what I knew was true, even if it couldn't be proven or if I'd never read it in books: that more comets flew than suns rose; that everyone slept on the job, so no one needed to apologize; that someone must have lined those apples up outside the fourth-floor bedroom window I couldn't budge, no matter how impossible it seemed. I had chameleoned into this life, or maybe it was the other way around. I stopped trying to distinguish anything from itself. I tried not to look at the moon directly. I stared at the bear suit piled in the corner and took off all my clothes.

Let Me Be Your Tugboat King

Listen, I'm ready for you to come right over here, darling, and dance with me. We're pulling in the weight of what we're waiting for. Dance it down for me. Let me see your sequins shimmer and shake. I want the breeze of all those sparkles to blow me right off this tugboat. We're getting down, all dancing equal, mismatched pulses, wanting nothing more than to keep moving and I?

I will be your tugboat king. I will call the do-si-dos, and the skip-to-my-lous. Hokey Cokey! Shimmy! Whip out a Watusi for me! We have flipped and landed decent. Now is when the crowd forms to clap and keep rhythm. No cardboard laid down, we are skull-spinning because that's what it'll take.

Turn the music up. It's time to move. Shake it out. Warn the neighbors: this'll go late. Ring that bell like pure silver. Swing it around. Here it comes: We're clear out of black and white into Technicolor: Set your eyes up for all this seeing.

Your tugboat king is doing the hustle, the Charleston: I'm ready to boogaloo: I'm foxtrotting: I'm locomoting, twisting, shouting: I'm working out a hully gully here: Do what I do.

Alcyone

I have this soul that's full of soil, and be honest: is there anything more terrifying than a stem showing up from the nowhere of below? My engagement stretches string thin. Someone gave out my lock combinations. My corners are chipped. The flesh beneath reveals a pleasant surprise. The beetles seem brighter in the pitch-black night. I am night. I am bells. I am tongues of noon. I watch a bee born in the quaintest moment. The body cancels the soul. I say prayers and rap on windows to be let in. I feel the shame slide through my smirk. I have a bruise the size of a handful. I populate men in a way that will surely someday be recognized. I sleep with skeptical ghosts. I carefully watch their mouths open. I frame babies with my body. I hang myself on others. Am I missing chances?

No, this feels nice: these mouths. I want to be banished. I want to return. I want to fascinate someone's ignorance. I want to shake coins from myself. I want to fill my bathing suit with corkscrews. I want to marrow and curdle. I want to smell of elderberry and hair. I want to watch the algae blossom on my bedpost. I want to feel the pain stutter up. I want to mourn, slow and plump. I want the battle to grow deep and homesick. Am I lost or found?

No, the lost are an invention of the finders. I have seen the clock, chalked and lisping. I have seen surgeons overcome by pieces of puzzles. I have adjusted, become all iris and anemone. I have been strange and inviting. My nerves have been my foes: a dull caper. I have written boring poems like thick thighs. I have watched the ceiling ride around the room. My mentors have torn my work apart like chicken bones. I have been cracked open, jacked off, spiraled up. Where am I now in this careful aging?

No, this is a becoming. This is a yearly debut. This ballroom black-foots. On the dance floor, I am a landlocked country. I am doused in limericks, needles, tatting. When you dance around me I become thumb knots and tack bends. I run stunt kites up into your hair with my hands. You glide joints. I celebrate High Holy Days. I fiddle your arms with my arms. I exhale like a rocking horse. My gown reveals me.

The Hush of the Party

There was once a lovely party held in the home of a wealthy baron.

This party was thrown when big parties were still a grand yet fathomable thing.

This party happened back when every woman's figure was enlarged by the concentric circles of the layers of her dress.

One would likely never encounter the best of one's friends at one of these parties because it was so crowded. They called this the "crush."

One reserved one's largest, most genuine smiles for those one didn't know.

A large stone terrace held men smoking thin cigarettes and women who pulled their delicate shawls more tightly around them.

This party took place before it became chivalrous to give a woman one's suit jacket to keep her warm.

To be so common as to need additional warmth from something so unfashionable as a suit jacket was unthinkable. One would certainly not have been invited back.

Conversations tittered on every balustrade.

Women in long black gloves leaned into the men with whom they spoke to whisper secrets behind their satiny fingers.

These men, so used to being coldly dismissed by the light of day, now well oiled with sherry and champagne and cognac, they placed daring hands on the arms, the shoulders, even the waists of girls who would then shift their body weight, apply the perfect amount of returning pressure.

Heads tilted down and eyes leaned up, the angles of seduction.

The conservatory was reserved for further flirtations.

It wasn't proper to dance more than twice with the same partner.

Old men spoke with choruses of widows. One outrageous comment would be boomed from a deep-barreled chest and a round of agreement, of embarrassed giggles, of silently smiling heads shaking would erupt from the audience of women who hadn't spoken to anyone besides their servants for days.

"How do you do?"

By the end of the night, trickles of wax decorated the men's epaulets. Such was the intoxication of the conversation, that they would be so carried away, driven to absent-mindedness, and converse under the dripping chandeliers.

The light of the room forecasted antiquity. The candles cast a sepia glow on the porcelain skin of men and women alike: these people who were used to waking at noon, dressing till two, and emerging for the society of the home just as the sun was setting behind old trees lining the path leading to the entrance.

Supper began at midnight.

A solitary wallflower, a genus that bred well in all ballrooms, broke into a conversation and reminded a man of his promise, showing him her dance card. He looked away from the bright young thing with whom he'd been talking and reassured the wallflower, "There'll be time enough for dancing."

She believed him; the night held so much.

Almost everyone had been to parties at the baron's home before, and weren't they all unsurprising? Didn't all of his parties feel just like all the other parties? Lovely to anticipate, even more enjoyable to recall at the next party, but just a present chore.

Hadn't someone said of the baron's last party that "the champagne was undrinkable," that "the pâte de foie gras tasted like kitten"? (And everyone had laughed, nodding, not asking the speaker how he knew the taste of kitten.)

The flowers flung into buttonholes this evening were mostly carnations, nothing particularly fancy.

The cane-bottomed benches that had been imported for extra seating remained empty all evening, only made the rooms smaller, pushed people closer together, farther from the walls. People remained on their feet, moving fluidly between groups. This was not an evening where one was always searching for a better conversation, but rather people couldn't contain themselves, talked over each other and at once. Every guest had a slew of things they wanted to say to many different people and all at the same time. So while couples grasped hands, shoulders, waists and counted the down up up one two three silently on the expansive dance floor, others in the parlor waltzed from cluster to cluster, touching down with a comment and then lifting in two steps to the next crowd, leaving a trail of riotous laughter behind, already evoking the next round from the imminent group.

After the seven waltzes came four galops, a polka, a polka-mazurka and then a quadrille to round the evening out.

Time passed both fast and slow. Things were just beginning as they were ending.

Walks proceeded through the garden. The satin hems of dresses would never be the same.

Amid all this bustle there was a time when everything got quiet, the chatter reduced to a whisper and the whole house hummed to the vaulted ceilings, through arcaded hallways, down through the marble floor and into the catacombs of cellars, where only a few wanton sneaks would traipse and stumble for a quick thrill. At this moment the house seemed at its fullest.

For everyone knows, no matter the visceral joy of laughing and story-telling, the great charm of a ball is its perfect accord and harmony—all altercations, loud talking, et cetera, are doubly ill-mannered in a ballroom. Very little suffices to disturb the peaces of the whole company.

As this party waged on, only the hissing and hushing S's of words were audible, as if all of the guests were telling each other to get quieter still.

The guests' mouths stretched around vowels that made no sound.

Everyone had returned inside from the chill of the night air.

They spoke through the dart and blink of their eyes.

One woman began to bend herself in a slow two-minute curtsy until the puddle of her dress stood higher than she.

All the women followed suit, curving, crooking, sliding into curtsies of their own.

The men matched the women before them with noble forty-five-degree bows.

The marble stones beneath the guests were spotless and sparkling as if a foot had yet to be set upon them.

For several minutes all anyone heard was the shallow, uneven breath, the push of rib cages against the whalebone stays of women's gowns as gravity seemed to work its slow pressure.

And soon silence, as everyone reached the nadir of their descent, pausing there.

One woman, hanging on the arm of an already silent man, pushed a French door open, her voice, sharp as a spoon chiming the rim of a wine glass, the last canary in the coal mine.

She looked around her and, finding everyone sunken, began to wind herself down as well. Her companion bent towards her.

Once they too had arrived at the depth of their poses, the silence was so exquisite that the crickets outside, too, must have laid down their heads for just the flicker of a moment.

Then all at once, the muscles eased into motion again, began the two-minute climb to cultivated posture.

Breath built to steady sighs of bliss. Words formed gracefully, careful not to crack the delicate crystal that hung in the air.

The energy built, pushed the ceiling higher, and what twinkled in everyone's eyes was the knowledge of why they attended balls in the first place: not to eat, or to dance, or to see their neighbors, but to remember and say that they had been there.

Acknowledgments

Thanks to the publications where these stories have previously appeared (sometimes under different names, in different forms): *A La Carte: Short Stories that Stir the Foodie in All of Us* "Recipe for Her Absence," *Another Chicago Magazine* "Twins, or Ambivalence," *bearcreekfeed* "The Tackiness of Souls," Bodega "Hammer, Damper," *Caketrain* "Like Lightning," *The Collagist* "The Grifted," *Dark Sky* "Engrossed" and "Entered," *Dewclaw* "Tangle," *Dogzplot* "Let Me Be Your Tugboat King," Featherproof as a mini-book and then *Cell Stories* "Hospitable Madness," *Frigg* "Madness is Doing the Same Thing Over and Over and Expecting Different Results," *Hotel St. George* "The Hush of the Party," *JMWW* "The Crickets Are Trying to Organize Themselves Into Some Raucous Pentameter," *Joyland* "The Chamber of the Enigma," *Juked* and *Best of the Web 2010* "Women in Wells," *Knee-Jerk* "Before We Pass This Way Again," *Lamination Colony* "A Willingness and a Warning," *Make Magazine* "Somebody Else's," *Midwestern Gothic* "More Mysteries," MLP as a mini-book "A Heaven Gone," *Nano Fiction* "Roundabout the Bottom," *Necessary Fiction* "Prowlers," Pank "The Things Which Blind Us," *Pear Noir* "Judgment Day," *Ping Pong* "The Direction of Forgetting," *Requited* "The Dark Spot," *Robot Melon* "Staying Alive During that Old War," *Six Sentences* "The Effects of Rotation," *Sleepingfish* "Felted," *SmokeLong* "Marbles Loosed," *Spork* "Unaccounted," *trnsfr* "Ratman," *Wag's Revue* "Filth and Rot," *Why Vandalism* "The Colleens," *Word Riot* "Half."

My greatest thanks go to Dan Wickett and Steven Gillis for giving these stories a second life and home. To Guy Intoci and Jeffery Gleaves for their incredible partnership and efforts, Michelle Dotter for the close eye, and Steven Seighman for the terrific design work. All gratitude to the hosts of the Chicago reading series, where many of these stories premiered, and the good old Dollar Store tour gang, for giving me reasons to write and the drive to write more and better, especially Aaron Burch, for reading this collection and talking to me about it. To all my professors and classmates at SAIC for making me think differently and better. Cheers to Claudia and what I hope will be a long collaboration. To all my family and friends for their understanding and support, especially my parents and sister for being models of dedication and love. And to Jared for always telling me to write instead.